A Book Of

ADVERTISING AND SALES PROMOTION

For

BBA Semester - VI

As Per New Syllabus w.e.f. 2015

Dr. Shaila Bootwala

M.Com., M.Phil, Ph.D. (Marketing)
Vice-Principal and Head, Dept. of Commerce
Abeda Inamdar Senior College
Pune

Asst. Prof. Fazil Mohammed Shareef

M.B.A.(Marketing) M.Com , NET

NIRALI PRAKASHAN
ADVANCEMENT OF KNOWLEDGE

N3467

Advertising and Sales Promotion (BBA - VI)   ISBN 978-93-5164-841-3

First Edition   :   December 2015
©   :   Authors

Published By :
NIRALI PRAKASHAN
Abhyudaya Pragati, 1312, Shivaji Nagar,
Off J.M. Road, PUNE – 411005
Tel - (020) 25512336/37/39, Fax - (020) 25511379
Email : niralipune@pragationline.com

✦ DISTRIBUTION CENTRES

PUNE

Nirali Prakashan   :   119, Budhwar Peth, Jogeshwari Mandir Lane, Pune 411002, Maharashtra
Tel : (020) 2445 2044, 66022708, Fax : (020) 2445 1538
Email : bookorder@pragationline.com, niralilocal@pragationline.com

Nirali Prakashan   :   S. No. 28/27, Dhyari, Near Pari Company, Pune 411041
Tel : (020) 24690204 Fax : (020) 24690316
Email : dhyari@pragationline.com, bookorder@pragationline.com

MUMBAI

Nirali Prakashan   :   385, S.V.P. Road, Rasdhara Co-op. Hsg. Society Ltd.,
Girgaum, Mumbai 400004, Maharashtra
Tel : (022) 2385 6339 / 2386 9976, Fax : (022) 2386 9976
Email : niralimumbai@pragationline.com

✦ DISTRIBUTION BRANCHES

JALGAON

Nirali Prakashan   :   34, V. V. Golani Market, Navi Peth, Jalgaon 425001,
Maharashtra, Tel : (0257) 222 0395, Mob : 94234 91860

KOLHAPUR

Nirali Prakashan   :   New Mahadvar Road, Kedar Plaza, 1st Floor Opp. IDBI Bank
Kolhapur 416 012, Maharashtra. Mob : 9850046155

NAGPUR

Pratibha Book Distributors   :   Above Maratha Mandir, Shop No. 3, First Floor,
Rani Jhanshi Square, Sitabuldi, Nagpur 440012, Maharashtra
Tel : (0712) 254 7129

DELHI

Nirali Prakashan   :   4593/21, Basement, Aggarwal Lane 15, Ansari Road, Daryaganj
Near Times of India Building, New Delhi 110002
Mob : 08505972553

BENGALURU

Pragati Book House   :   House No. 1, Sanjeevappa Lane, Avenue Road Cross,
Opp. Rice Church, Bengaluru – 560002.
Tel : (080) 64513344, 64513355,Mob : 9880582331, 9845021552
Email:bharatsavla@yahoo.com

CHENNAI

Pragati Books   :   9/1, Montieth Road, Behind Taas Mahal, Egmore,
Chennai 600008 Tamil Nadu, Tel : (044) 6518 3535,
Mob : 94440 01782 / 98450 21552 / 98805 82331,
Email : bharatsavla@yahoo.com

niralipune@pragationline.com | www.pragationline.com

Also find us on [f] www.facebook.com/niralibooks

Dedication ...

This book is dedicated to

"ADAMYA SHARMA"

Welcome to the family

Dr. Shaila Bootwala

Preface ...

It gives us immense pleasure in presenting this book of marketing titled 'Advertising and Sales Promotion' This book has been written keeping in mind the New Syllabus proposed by The Board of studies in marketing, for B.B.A. final year students of Marketing specialisation.

It covers the entire syllabus comprehensively and deals with minute concepts very clearly. Great effort has been made to define the salient features realistically and practically. The book will provide an overall understanding of Advertising and Sales Promotion. The topics relate to Measurement of Effective Advertising, Copy Decisions, Media Decisions, Sales Promotion and Brand Equity and Role of Information Technology in Advertising and Sales Promotion.

We would like to thank our family and friends for being a constant support in this Endeavour to present this book to you.

We are very grateful to Shri. Dinesh bhai Furia, Shri. Jigneshbhai Furia, our publishers, for providing us with this opportunity and the entire staff of Nirali Prakashan for their support. A special word of appreciation for Supriya Singh, who has been instrumental in getting this book to the stands. We would also like to express our thanks Mr. Akbar Sheikh for his co-operation.

We shall consider our hard work amply rewarded if this book is appreciated by those for whom it is meant. We extend all our good wishes to the students, teachers and readers whose valuable and constructive suggestions would be welcome to improve this book.

Prof. Dr. Shaila Bootwala
Asst. Prof. Mohd. Fazil Shareef

Syllabus ...

1. **Introduction and Measurement of Effective Advertising**
   1.1 Advertising: Evolution, Meaning, Definition, Classification, Benefits, Functions, Criticism, Ethics, Social issues.
   1.2 Strategic Advertising Decision: Setting Advertising Objectives, Deciding Advertising Budget, Advertising Framework Planning and Organization
   1.3 Advertising Campaign: Meaning, Basis of Campaign, Length of Campaign, Parameters governing advertising Campaign, Planning of advertising of Campaign
   1.4 Advertising Agency: Meaning, Definition, Functions, Types, Advantages, Structure, Advertiser and Advertising Interface.
   1.5 Advertising Effectiveness: Objective of measuring Advertising Effectiveness, Difficulties and Evaluation of Advertising Effectiveness
   1.6 Advertising Control: Control of Advertising by Practitioners

2. **Copy Decisions:**
   2.1 Advertising Copy: Meaning, Objectives, Elements, Features, Types of Copy
   2.2 Advertising Layout: Principles, Components, Visualization of Layout, Layout Format,
   2.3 Copy Creation: Approaches, Principles, Styles of Copy creation, Verbal Versus Visual Thinking, Pre Testing Methods and Measurements

3. **Media Decisions:**
   3.1 Advertising Media: Meaning, Definition, Functions, Types of Media
   3.2 Media Planning: Importance, Process, Difficulties, Basics of Reach, Frequency, Continuity in Media Planning.
   3.3 Media Research: Meaning, Importance, Functions, Process of Media Research
   3.4 Media Selection: Approaches and factors affecting Media Selection.

4. **Sales Promotion and Brand Equity:**
   4.1 Sales Promotion: Meaning, Definition, Objectives of Sales promotion, Factors affecting Sales Promotion Growth, Techniques of Sales Promotion
   4.2 Strategic Sales Promotion: Strategies and Practices in Sales Promotion, Cross Promotions, Surrogate Selling, Bait and Switch Advertising Issues.
   4.3 Brand Equity: Concepts and Criteria, Building, Measuring and Managing Brand Equity, Linking Advertising and Sales promotion to achieve "Brand Standing", Leveraging Brand values for business and non-business contexts.

5. **Role of Information Technology in Advertising and Sales Promotion:**
   5.1 Comparison of Traditional and Modern Advertising
   5.2 Internet Advertising: Purpose, Types, Advantages, disadvantages of internet Advertising
   5.3 Pre-requisites of Online Advertising
   5.4 E-Advertising Guidelines
   5.5 Internet Advertising today

Contents ...

Chapter **1**...

Introduction and Measurement of Effective Advertising

Contents ...

Learning Objectives ...

- To understand the meaning, nature and scope of advertising
- To study the advertising objectives and the role of advertising in modern business
- To learn the meaning and importance of ethics in advertising
- To explain the various functions of advertising
- To elaborate on the benefits and limitations of advertising

1.1 Advertising

1.1.1 Introduction

When a marketer or a firm has developed a product to satisfy the market demand, there is a need for establishing contact with the target market so as to sell the product. Moreover, this has to be a mass contact as the marketer is interested in reaching out to a large number of people. Naturally the best way to reach this mass market is through mass communication, and advertising is one of the means of such mass communication along with other means such as publicity, sales promotion and public relations.

The term 'advertising' is derived from the Latin word 'advertere' which means 'to turn' the attention. Today all round us we see advertising turning the attention of everyone towards a particular product, service or area. Advertising is a means of mass communication and has made mass selling possible. Advertising is a means of forceful mass communication, which promotes the sale of goods, services and ideas through information and persuasion. Here it should be noted that advertising only draws the public towards the particular product service or idea. Repeated sales will take place only if the consumer finds the product satisfactory. Thus advertising only helps in selling.

1.1.2 Meaning and Definition of Advertising

The most widely accepted definition of advertising is the one given by the **'American Marketing Association'**, which is "*Advertising is any paid form of non-personal presentation of ideas, goods or services by an identified sponsor*".

This definition highlights the following aspects of advertising.

1. **Any form:** Advertising is any form of communication. It may be a symbol or sign, an illustration or an ad message in a magazine, or newspaper. It may be a commercial on television or radio, or a circular dispatched through the mail. Advertising can take any of these and other forms also.

2. **Paid form:** This means that advertising is a commercial transaction and has to be paid for.

3. **Non-personal:** This phrase in the definition excludes personal selling from within the scope of advertising. Advertising has to be non-personal that is, addressed to a mass audience. Thus person-to-person presentation is not advertising.

4. **Identified sponsor:** This means that the sponsor of the advertisement openly pays for it.

In other words advertising is a sales message directed at a mass audience, which seeks to sell goods, services and ideas on behalf of a paying sponsor through the use of persuasion.

In a nutshell, advertising is a mass communication process of persuading the prospects by convincing them to buy products or services with increased satisfaction to the consumers and profits to the sponsors.

1.1.3 Nature and Elements

Advertising is a mass communication of information intended to persuade buyers to buy products and with a view to maximising a company's profits. Elements of advertising are:

1. It is a mass communication reaching a large group of consumers.

2. It makes mass production possible.

3. It is non-personal communication, for an actual person does not deliver it, nor is it addressed to a specific person.

4. It is a commercial communication because it is used to help assure the advertiser of a long business life with profitable sales.

5. Advertising can be economical, for it reaches a large number of people.

6. The advertising communication is speedy, permitting an advertiser to speak to millions of buyers within a matter of few minutes.

7. Advertising is identified communication. The advertiser signs his name on his advertisement for the purpose of publicising his identity.

However it is important to note that advertising is not an exact science. The circumstance of each advertiser differs from others. He cannot predict with exact accuracy what will be the results of his present and future advertising efforts.

Advertising is not a game. But if it is done properly both the seller and the buyer tend to gain.

Advertising is not a toy. Advertisers cannot afford to play with advertising. They realise that advertising funds come from sales revenue and must be used to increase sales revenue.

Advertisements should not be designed to deceive. Apart from ethics, the desire for repeated sales ensures a high degree of honesty in advertising.

1.1.4 Scope

Advertising consists of those activities by which visual or oral messages are addressed to a selected public for the purpose of informing and influencing them to buy products or services, or to act favourably towards ideas, persons, trademarks or institutions featured. As contrasted with publicity and other forms of propaganda, advertising messages are identified with the advertiser either by signature or oral statement. Further, advertising is a commercial transaction and involves payments to be made to publishers, broadcasters or others whose media are employed.

The scope of advertising can be better understood by dividing all promotional activities into two; activities included in advertising and activities excluded from advertising. Let us take up the first part.

1. Activities included in advertising: Advertising usually includes the following forms of messages; the messages carried in newspapers and magazines, on outdoor boards, on street cars, rickshaws, trains, posters and painted displays, in radio and television broadcasts, and in circulars of all kinds, whether distributed by mail or person, through tradesmen or by inserts in packages, dealer-help materials, window display and counter display materials and efforts, store signs, house organs when directed to dealers and consumers, motion pictures used for advertising and novelties bearing advertising messages or signature of the advertiser. Labels, tags and other literature accompanying merchandise are also deemed to be advertising.

2. Activities excluded from advertising: The activities excluded from advertising include the offering of premiums to stimulate the sale of products, the use of exhibitions and demonstrations at fairs, shows, and conventions; the use of samples, and the so called "publicity activities" involved in the sending out of news releases. Likewise totally excluded from the advertising activity is the activity of the personal selling force, the payment of advertising allowances that are not used for advertising, and the entertainment of customers.

Often these activities excluded from the scope of advertising are included in the advertising budgets, and directed by those in charge of advertising. On many there is close room for argument whether they should be called as advertising or otherwise classified. They have been excluded from the scope of advertising for one reason or another. For example, exhibitions and demonstrations at fairs and shows are thought to be more closely related to personal selling than to advertising.

1.1.5 Evolution of Advertising

Though advertising, as we understand it today, was not used till about 200 years ago, as a business tool it is not new. It has the longest history taking us back to the history of mankind and the human civilisation. Though we fail to answer the question as to the exact age of advertising, it can be said that advertising began when man discovered the art of communication. Advertising by word of mouth is probably the earliest form of advertising, as man developed oral skills well before the development of reading and writing. The history of advertising can be studied by its progress through the centuries.

1. **Ancient Times up to the 5ᵗʰ Century**

    The use of advertising for the transmission of information dates back to ancient Greece and Rome. Criers and signs were used to carry information about goods and services well before the development of printing. During this time merchants used to identify their places of business with a symbol that told of their trade. Thus shop signs, as a means of identifying the place of business, are a relic of this time. During these times the merchants also used "hired criers" or "barkers" to impress upon the customers the quality of their products.

2. **The Dark Age**

    The period from 465 AD to 800 AD is referred to as "The Dark Age". This is the period that starts with the downfall of the Roman Empire and ends with the coronation of Charlemagne. During this period due to the fall of the Roman Empire business suffered a severe setback and commerce and trade routes were greatly diminished. Hence one does not hear much of advertising during this period. This does not mean that it dried up totally. Public barkers equipped with horns and bells were used to attract the attention of the public and hand executed signs and placards were used during this period too.

3. **The Middle Age**

    During this middle ages, advertising signs were very extensively used. Criers for the taverns were so numerous in Paris in the 13th century that they formed a union and were chartered by King Philip Augustus. The giving of free samples started during this era by these criers. Printing originated in China and the oldest book printed dates back to 868 AD. In 1438, Johann Gutenberg laid the foundation of modern education inventing a system of casting moveable type, in Germany and printed the famous Bible in 1456. This discovery, in the West was the first leap for advertising. New methods of advertising were now available like printed posters, hand-bills, pamphlets and newspapers.

4. **The 16th and 17th Centuries**

This was the time when the printing technique was perfected, and newspapers were introduced. The first newspapers were in the form of newsletters. The early advertisements in the newspapers were in the form of announcements. Importers of new products to England made these announcements. For example the first advertisement offering coffee was made in a newspaper in England in 1652. Chocolates and tea were first introduced through newspaper ads in 1657 and 1658 respectively in England. The earlier advertisements in the newspapers were for books, marriage offers, new beverages and ads for travel. Initially advertising in newspapers was primarily "pioneering advertising" in its nature. Competitive advertising came in much later in the 18th century in England.

5. **The 18th and 19th Centuries**

This period witnessed the birth and blossoming of competitive advertising. Space selling came into existence. Around 1840, several people were selling space in newspapers in New York. Now there was no looking back. The age-old principle of 'caveat emptor' ruled the transactions. Advertising was not only competitive but also had an untruthful edge to it. That is why people did not totally believe the advertising messages given. Buyers were cautious and diligent in buying advertised goods. The 19th century was marked by a new trend of brand advertising. Magazines started catching the imagination of people by popularising brands. This is the period during which 'point of purchase' advertising became popular.

6. **The 20th Century**

The 20th century saw the discovery of the radio, television and satellite communications. It has witnessed the world shrink into one global village. With this advertising has received a major boost as never before. New, different anti-vibrant advertisements are the order of the day. Advertisements can be viewed and heard across the length and breadth of the world. They can be heard on radio, seen and heard on TV, videos, computer, CDs, internet, as well as hoardings, newspapers, magazines etc. The era of information technology and mass communication has so developed that business without advertising is a virtual impossibility. Competitive advertisements and advertising wars are a regular feature of normal business life. The success and failure of a business is decided to a large extent by its advertising strategy.

7. **The 21ˢᵗ Century:**

The 21ˢᵗ century has seen mass inroads being made by the internet. It has changed the definition of literacy. Today a person who has no knowledge of computer and the internet is deemed to be an illiterate. The 21ˢᵗ century has also seen the mobile phone percolate to every corner of the world and to every strata of society. SMS and MMS are the new forms of advertising. A plethora of mobile apps today compete for the attention of the mobile phone user. Right from games to shopping to location of restaurants and theatres, there are apps available for almost everything.

Thus the advertising industry started with "barkers" and has culminated into a very powerful mass media of communication that targets individual users through the mobile phone. It is an industry at the very core of all businesses, and something without which no business can exist.

1.1.6 Classification/Types of Advertising

Advertising can be basically classified into two categories.

1.   Product-related Advertising

2.   Institutional Advertising

1. **Product-related Advertising**

As the name implies, it is concerned with conveying information about, and selling a product or service. Product advertising is of three types.

(i)   **Pioneering Advertising:** Pioneering advertising is concerned with developing a "primary" demand – that is conveying information about and selling a product category rather than a specific brand. The initial advertising for vacuum cleaners, microwave ovens etc. are of this nature. This kind of advertising is used when a new product is just introduced in the market. This type of advertising is used in the introductory stages in the lifecycle of a product. This kind of advertising may have different advertising objectives like, conveying information, selling the product idea etc. An example of pioneering advertising is the advertisement of the Tea Board of India promoting the idea of tea as a health drink.

(ii)   **Competitive Advertising:** This type of advertising seeks to stimulate "selective" demand. It is useful when the product has reached the growth, or more especially the maturity stage. This advertising seeks to sell a specific brand rather than a general product category. Competitive advertising is of two types.

(a)   **Direct Type/Direct-Action Advertising:** This type of advertising seeks to stimulate direct buying action. Its main objective is to seek an immediate response to the advertisement in the form of the readers sending an order for the goods advertised or a request for further information.

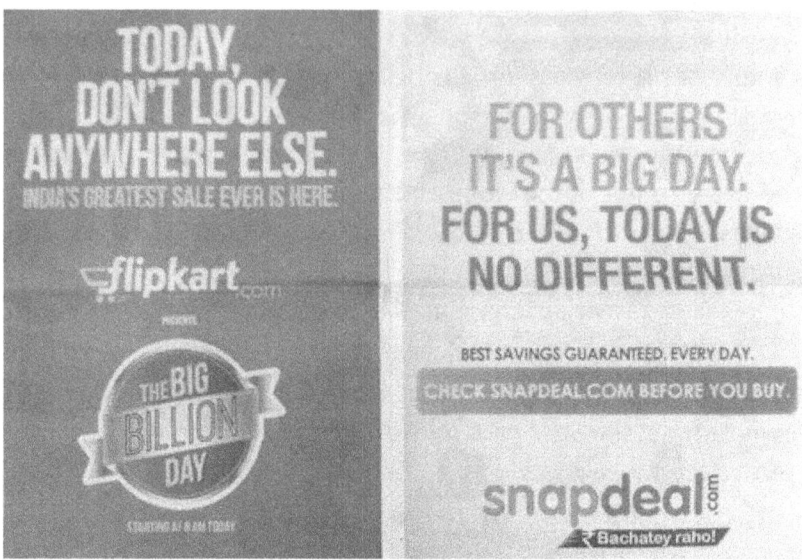

Fig. 1.1

(b) Indirect Type/Indirect-Action Advertising: Indirect-action advertisements do not seek an immediate response from the reader. Their objective is to build the reputations of the brands advertised and to enhance the desirability of the branded products offered by pinpointing the virtues of the product. The objective of doing all this is that all this will affect the consumer's action, and when he is ready to buy the product, he will buy the advertised brand.

Fig. 1.2

Fig. 1.3

(iii) **Retentive Advertising:** This may be useful when the product has achieved a favourable status in the market, that is, when it has attained maturity. Here the advertiser wants to keep the name of his product before the public. A much softer selling approach is used, or only the name may be mentioned in "reminder" type of advertising. The main objective of this type is to remind the people about the availability of the product.

2. Institutional Advertising

Institutional advertising as contrasted with product advertising is devoted to building goodwill for the company. This type of advertising sells only the name and prestige of the company. Large companies with many divisions, whose various products are well known, frequently use this kind of institutional advertising.

Institutional advertising is used extensively during periods of product shortages in order to keep the name of the company before the public. Some large companies also use institutional advertising to encourage consumers of the desirability of large companies.

Institutional advertising is designed to create a positive attitude towards the seller of the product or services. Such an advertisement does not sell the product but creates goodwill for the seller or manufacturer in the market. The objective of this advertisement is not to sell a product but to establish a high level of goodwill. Institutional advertising can be further sub-divided into three areas. They are:

(i) **Public Relations Institutional Advertising:** Public relations institutional advertising attempts to create a favourable image of the firm among employees, stockholders or the general public; for example, the television advertisement of Telco showing its commitment towards excellence and its caring attitude towards its workers.

(ii) **Public Service Institutional Advertising:** This is directed at the social welfare of a community or a nation. The effectiveness of a public service advertisement may be measured in terms of the goodwill it generates in favour of the sponsoring organisation. Public service institutional advertising can be illustrated by advertisements urging people to donate blood, donate eyes, adopt a child, AIDS awareness, family planning and population control, road safety, child labour etc. The objective of this type of advertising is not only to inform the public and get them to behave in a particular way that is beneficial for society, but also to earn goodwill for the sponsoring company.

Fig. 1.4

(iii) **Patronage Institutional Advertising** is designed to attract customers by emphasising a patronage-buying motive rather than a product-buying motive. For example a retailer might inform the public about his extended hours of work, open 7 days a week, or a manufacturer may advertise his new warranty policy. Some other patronage motives that can be used in such advertisements are good location, good service, free delivery etc. The objective of this kind of an advertisement is to draw customers towards that particular outlet.

1.1.7 Benefits of Advertising

(A) Consumers and Advertising/Benefits of Advertising to the Consumer

The ultimate aim of all marketing efforts is to satisfy the needs of the consumers by transferring the benefits of productive efficiency to the final users. Advertising as an important element in this process of transfer helps consumers in the following ways.

1. **Advertising adds perception utility to the product:** Advertising adds perception utility to the product just as manufacturing adds form utility, transportation adds place utility and warehousing adds time utility. Advertising influences the perception of the consumers about the product by pointing out the various benefits to be derived from its use. Thus it creates a desire in the mind of the consumers to purchase the product.

2. **Advertising helps the consumer in making the purchase decision:** Advertising through its various forms gives out useful information about the relative merits and features of the products and services in terms of price, quality, utility, quantity, durability, convenience of use etc. so as to guide the consumers to select a product or service of a particular sponsor. As advertising brings to the fore the various features of the various available products, the consumer can compare the merits of the various products and come to a purchase decision. Thus the process of decision-making is made easier.

3. **Advertising ensures a better quality:** Advertising ensures that customers are drawn to the product at least for a trial order. However repeat orders are placed only due to the satisfaction received through the use of the product. Thus if the product is not good, repeat sales will not take place and if the product proves to be good it will imprint an image on the minds of the customers and earn a long-standing reputation for the manufacturing house. Such an image is possible by effective branding. Manufacturers are desirous not only of this image but of repeat sales and hence, advertising ensures better quality products to the consumers.

4. **Goods at reasonable prices:** Advertising enables firms to sell goods on a mass scale. This has made it possible for producers to increase their production so as to earn economies of scale and thus they can offer goods at reasonable prices to consumers.

5. **Better standard of living:** Advertising reduces the prices of products and thus more and more products are affordable by a larger section of society today. Thus it increases the standard of living of the people. Further advertising creates a demand for new products and thus increases the standard of living of the masses.

6. **Time saved in shopping:** Advertising increases the knowledge of the consumers about the availability of the various brands in the market. They get to know about the products and services of the different producers and as such it saves their time which would otherwise have been spent in locating, identifying and deciding about the products and services.

7. **Advertising contributes to consumer welfare:** Advertising helps consumers in a variety of ways. It tells them what to buy, how to buy, where to buy and why to buy. It also gives valuable price information. Advertising also promotes consumer welfare by encouraging competition, which leads to improvements in product quality and reduction in prices.

8. **Advertising makes consumers think:** Advertising makes consumers aware of many socially relevant causes like dowry, energy conservation, environmental pollution, child marriages, eye and blood donation etc. Advertising thus not only makes a consumer think, but acts as a friend, philosopher and guide to the consumers.

(B) Manufacturers and Advertising/Benefits of Advertising to the Manufacturer

Manufacturers, who make available their goods with the clear intention of disposing them at a profit to themselves and satisfaction to the customers, take full advantage of advertising as a major tool to popularise their products and services. Manufacturers spend a lot on advertising because it pays to do so. Advertising establishes a link between the manufacturer and the consumer. It is a form of mass communication. Through this form, the manufacturer makes his product offering known to the consumers. Advertising helps the manufacturer to get the following benefits.

1. **Advertising creates customers:** Even if the producer manufactures the best product, he cannot sell it without advertising. Even though it is said that *"a good wine needs no bush"*, information about the product should reach those interested in buying it. Thus it is advertising that informs the people about the product and creates a demand for it.

2. **Advertising increases the sales:** In a highly sensitive and competitive market, the profits of the firm can be maximised not only by reducing the costs but by increasing the sales. Sales of the firm can be multiplied by advertising. Thus advertising increases sales.

3. **Advertising helps the producer in informing the market about the changes in the product or service:** In our competitive system it is important for a manufacturer who has innovated a new product or service, to tell the public about the same quickly in order to reap the advantages right from the start before the competition can develop a similar product. Advertising helps the manufacturer to do this.

4. **Advertising controls product prices:** Through advertising, it is possible to control the prices of the products, specially the retail prices. Very often greedy retailers exploit needy consumers by charging higher prices. Advertising stops this exploitation by disclosing the maximum retail price of the product.

5. **Advertising acts as a salesman:** What a travelling salesman does for the manufacturer, advertising does at a lesser cost. Salesmen have to be fed, paid a salary and provided with an expense account. Contrast this with the cost of selling through advertising. A national advertisement, once the original cost has been paid, may reach millions of prospects. There are no expense accounts and an advertisement carried by radio or television reaches into every remote corner of the country. Thus advertising not only acts as a salesman, but also reduces the selling cost of the manufacturer.

6. **Advertising widens the market:** Advertising is an important tool that can open the doors of national and international markets. Intensive advertising programmes conducted by a manufacturer give him wider markets for his products.

(C) Salesman and Advertising/Benefits of Advertisings to the Salesman

Sales of an organisation happen because of the active involvement of two functions. First the salesman makes sales happen through his direct personal efforts, and secondly advertising leads to sales through indirect efforts. Which of these two is more important cannot be said, as a company has to match the efforts of both so as to achieve maximum sales. However, salesmen benefit from advertising in the following ways.

1. **Advertising creates a colourful background for the salesman:** A salesman is nothing less than an actor who by his skill and mastery over the art of selling, tries to win over the consumers for the products of his company. All his selling skills are more effective when they are performed against a good and colourful background. Advertising creates this background for the salesman and thus his job is made more effective.

2. **Advertising makes the salesman's job easier:** In the absence of advertising the salesman has to perform a double job; that of introducing the product to the consumer and then creating a need, want and desire in the mind of the consumer for the product. But because of advertising the customer is already aware about the product and to a certain extent need, want and desire have already been created. Thus the work of the salesman becomes much easier as advertising sells between the sales calls.

3. **Advertising instils confidence in the salesman:** Advertising creates an image and goodwill for the company, which in turn instils a feeling of pride amongst the salesmen that they are working for such an esteemed organisation. This feeling of pride instils in them self-confidence and makes them a dynamic and intrinsically motivated workforce.

(D) Benefits of Advertising to Society

Advertising is not just a business activity that results in only profits and losses, but affects society at large. In fact everyone in society tends to be affected by it. Following are some of the benefits of advertising that are reaped by the society at large.

1. **Advertising increases the standard of living of the society:** The standard of living of the society is conditioned by the amount of national income and its distribution on the one hand, and the consumption pattern and the disposable income on the other hand. The generation of national income is deeply influenced by advertising. This is because, effective and faithful advertising creates a demand, which in turn puts pressure on the wheels of production not only to produce more but also to produce

better and cheaper products keeping an eye on the quality standards. Improvement in standard of living implies increased production, better production and cheaper production, thus making more and more people from the lower income brackets to enjoy the products they could not in the past.

2. **Advertising provides employment opportunities:** Advertising creates oppor-tunities for gainful employment, both directly and indirectly. Directly employment opportunities are available in the various branches of this ever-growing field of advertising. This profession requires the services of various specialists and talented people like artists, painters, photographers, content editors, singers, musicians, executives, agents, researchers etc. Indirectly it stimulates the production of goods, which in turn creates employment opportunities.

3. **Advertising reflects and affects the culture of the society in which it operates:** Culture stands for the values of life and living. Each race has a different culture. Culture is always changing and is guided by the dynamics of the social, political and ethical dimensions of the people. Advertising simply reflects the culture of the people; it does not create it. It simply responds to the prevailing value system. The advertiser has to know very minutely the attitudes, beliefs and motives of the target audience. He then selects the appropriate media, advertisement messages etc. Advertisers are interested in a favourable response from the target audience, and this would be possible only when they offer, in the form of advertisements, products and services that fit into the existing value system of the audience.

   Not only does advertising reflect the culture of the people, but it, in its turn, also affects the culture. It does not create culture but definitely is responsible for changes in culture. Advertising is a very dynamic and influential force. In fact, the current world is moving on the lever of advertising. With its educative value, provoking force and invoking tinge, it affects thoughts, gestures and behaviour of the people caught in the spotlight of advertising. Consumers' attitudes, habits, likes and dislikes, fashions, actions, in every walk of life are deeply influenced by advertising.

4. **Advertising provides information to the masses:** Advertising educates the public. Each advertisement is a piece of information because each advertising copy has a definite theme behind it. Advertisements carry messages to different sections of society. They carry the ideas, views and opinions of different people and thus provide information to the masses. It is through advertising that an employer fills the vacancies in his firm. An unemployed applies for a job, parents hunt for brides and bridegrooms, the government appeals to the public to pay their tax dues, various NGOs appeal to the public about various socially relevant causes, film producers speak of their films, cinema houses remind us of regular and special shows. Thus, advertising definitely informs the masses.

1.1.8 Functions of Advertising

Advertising can be said to perform the following functions.

1. **Information Function:** Advertising is essentially a form of mass communication. As such, its primary responsibility is to deliver the relevant information to a specific audience.

Fig. 1.5

2. **Precipitation Function:** Advertising moves a consumer closer to buying a product in a step-by-step fashion; from being totally unaware of the product to buying it. Advertising is effective if it moves a consumer a step along the purchase process. This function of advertising is known as the precipitation function. In order to understand this function better, let us understand the process of purchase that a consumer has to go through. There are many such processes. However, one that has stood the test of time well was developed by **Lavidge** and **Steiner**. According to them, people go through seven steps to reach the threshold of purchase.

These seven steps are:

(i)   Unawareness of goods or service,

(ii)   Awareness of the product,

(iii)   Knowledge of what the product offers,

(iv)   Liking for or a favourable attitude towards the product,

(v)   A preference for one brand over others,

(vi)   A desire to buy the product and a conviction that buying it would be wise, and

(vii)   Purchase.

Thus the precipitation function of advertising is to move people up a step on the ladder of purchase. Hence, an ad is effective if it moves a person from unawareness of the product to awareness. The steps in this hierarchy are not necessarily equidistant from each other. And consumers can move up several steps simultaneously. In its simplest form this model assumes that all consumers start from scratch, however some consumers have a negative attitude which must be changed before they can move up the steps.

Fig. 1.6

3. **Persuasive Function:** Another function of advertising is to persuade the consumers to move towards the point of purchase. That is, an advertisement should persuade people to purchase the product. This process of moving consumers to purchase may take minutes, hours, months or even years. But it is the ultimate goal of all advertising. An ad may persuade by appealing to emotions such as love or fear or rational motives such as savings or quality.

Fig. 1.7

4. **Reinforcement Function:** By making people feel good about their previous decisions to buy a product, advertising serves a reinforcement function. Such advertisements reinforce in the minds of the customers that their decision to purchase was the right one. Such advertisements usually portray a consumer research as ranking their product No. 1. For example, the Wagon R advertisement claims "The

Wagon R is rated best by customers two times over". Such ads may also use testimonials to reinforce the decision of the customers.

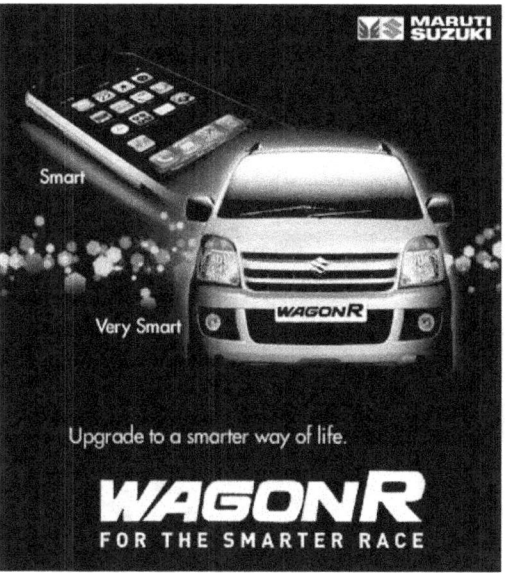

Fig. 1.8

5. **Reminder Function:** Another function of advertising is to remind the consumer about the availability of the product. Usually reminder ads that are intended to keep the advertiser's name fresh in the minds of the target audience perform this function. Through repetition and minimal text such as the Himani Gold Soap television advertisement remind the people and provide top-of-the-mind awareness about the product.

Fig. 1.9

6. **Value-Adding Function:** It is common knowledge that consumers perceive brands as more and more similar. Trying to establish brand loyalty in an era when this behaviour is rapidly eroding has proven to be one of the challenges facing marketers. Experts agree that advertising is still the most effective method of nurturing a brand's image over a long period. Thus, a function of advertising is to increase the perceived value of a brand through advertising. Such ads have the capability of endowing a brand with a symbolic meaning that makes it more valuable in the eyes of the consumers. According to this reasoning, a consumer will choose a brand of baby food when it conveys the image of a nurturing parent, select a brand of Cola when it is tied to a positive group identification, buy a brand of running shoe for its ability to communicate fitness or purchase an expensive automobile because it communicates affluence. Thus, advertising through the way it projects the particular products, adds a perceived value to it for the consumer.

Fig. 1.10

1.1.9 Criticisms of Advertising

1. **Advertising compels people to buy things they do not need:** Advertising is a mass communication that persuades people to buy. Thus attractive advertising creates a desire in the minds of the people even for those goods which they do not actually need thus getting them to purchase products that are not necessary.

2. **Advertising is a prime source of discontent:** Some critics of advertising point out that the prime source of discontent today is advertising. This argument claims that were it not for advertising, we would all be less aware of the material things that are to be had in this world and we would therefore feel greater content.

3. **It increases the cost of goods:** Modern advertising is a gigantic effort at mass persuasion. If it is not properly conducted, there is a possibility that huge amounts of wastes in terms of money, energy, time and space will take place. It is this waste that increases the cost of goods. Every waste in advertising reduces its effectiveness and sometimes even renders it completely useless. There are many reasons why such waste arises in advertising efforts. Some of the important reasons responsible for waste in advertising are as under:

(a) Wrong targeting

(b) Wrong direction

(c) Wrong selection of media

(d) Wrong time chosen for advertising

(e) Wrong policy

(f) Wrong use of space

To some extent waste is inevitable. However, some waste like waste due to poor design of an ad campaign can be eliminated totally by entrusting the job to a professional agency.

Another major reason for advertising increasing the cost of goods is competitive advertising expenditure after saturation of demand has been reached. Such competitive advertising expenditure does not increase the sale of the product. However, the expenditure has to take place as the competition is doing the same. Such expenditure just adds to the cost and makes goods costlier.

4. **It is false, deceptive and misleading:** Another criticism of advertising is that, it many a times makes untruthful and false claims leading to a sale and the dissatisfaction of the consumer. Another aspect of deception in advertising is the perception it creates about the product in the minds of the consumer. The reality of the product then does not live up to this perception and leads to dissatisfaction in the customer or affects his buying behaviour negatively.

5. **It is vulgar in taste:** Some of the critics of advertising say that it is vulgar in the sense that there is too much of emphasis on the sex appeal. Another criticism is the unnecessary use of women in some advertisements. Many television advertisements are repulsive to the most liberal minds. Advertisements are noisy, abrasive, often ill-timed and on occasion, stupid. It is undeniably true that advertising, at one time or another irritates almost everyone.

6. **It tends to develop monopolies:** Advertising gives rise to monopolies by creating a strong brand preference. Well-planned and effective advertising can make a marketer a leader in the market with more than 60% market share. Further advertising can

create monopolies as a big firm can undertake very heavy advertising expenditure thus forcing the small firms out of the market, or making their entry very difficult. Thus Surf Washing Powder ruled the washing powder market for a very long period. So did Colgate Dental Cream as it was a recognised market leader in the toothpaste market.

But, however powerful the monopoly is, it cannot be perpetual. It has to break. Colgate has been pushed out from its position as market leader and today a number of toothpaste brands are vying for the attention of the consumer. Similarly Surf also had to give in and make place for other washing powders entering the market. The reason for the break in monopoly situation is that there is no monopoly over ideas. Similar products do turn out and break the monopoly. Similarly, there is no monopoly over the media. Hence, there cannot be absolute monopoly through advertising.

7. **Advertising leads to product proliferation:** Advertising leads to the multiplication of products that are almost identical resulting in wastage of resources which could otherwise have been used to produce other products.

8. **Inefficient manufacturers stay in business:** One of the short-term effects of advertising is that, it can enable inefficient manufacturers to sell their sub-standard products by extensive advertising and thus stay in business. This is detrimental to consumers, if they can be lured by advertising into buying low quality products.

Even though the above criticism of advertising does exist to some extent, and cannot be denied, we have to accept the fact that communicating to consumers about the vast variety of products and services available is next to impossible without advertising. Advertising is in fact one of the important paths on which modern day society revolves.

1.1.10 Ethical and Social Issues in Advertising

To understand what ethical advertising is, we must understand what is unethical advertising. According to one market survey, advertising is considered unethical when:

1. It degrades the rival's product or substitute product.
2. It gives misleading information.
3. It gives false information.
4. It conceals information that vitally affects human life (for example, side-effects of drugs).
5. It makes exaggerated claims.
6. It is obscene or immoral.
7. It is against national and public interest.
8. Endorsements of products by celebrities who are opinion leaders is also sometimes criticised for spreading falsehood.

Ethical advertising contains truth, not absolute truth, but socially accepted standards of honesty as truth. It has to be right in its approach and claims. An advertising communication is a mix of art and facts within the scope of ethical principles. In order to be consumer oriented, an advertisement will have to be truthful and ethical. An advertisement should not mislead the consumer. If this happens its credibility will be lost. Its goodwill will be lost, not only for this product but possibly for the entire product range. However, truth in advertising should be valued for its own sake. Remember, unethical advertising is bad for business.

Advertising truth is to be viewed from the consumers' point of view and not in the narrow legalistic framework.

However, many a times it is a very difficult task to judge what is true and what is untrue. But, an advertisement as such is judged by its impact and from its acceptance by the consumers. What it promises must be there in the performance of the product, for it to be true and ethical.

In short, advertising is a social force and hence must honour the time-tested norms of social behaviour. It should not be an affront on people's moral sense.

1. Deceptive Advertising/Harmful Effects/Confuses the People

Conceptually, deception exists when an advertisement is introduced into the perceptual process of some audience and the output of that perceptual process (1) differs from the reality of the situation, and (2) affects buying behaviour to the detriment of the consumer. The input itself may be determined to contain falsehood. The more difficult and perhaps more common case, however, is when the input, that is, the advertisement, is not obviously false but the perceptual process generates an impression which is deceptive. A disclaimer may not pass through the attention filter of the audience or the message may be misinterpreted. Thus, deception refers not only to the information content in the advertisement but may also arise from misplaced emphasis in presentation.

Take the example of the television advertisement of the toothpaste "Meswak". It portrays one lady telling another the benefits of Meswak. The advertisement talks of various ways in which Meswak can be good for the health of a person. A consumer may get carried away with all these benefits, buy the product and then realise that it is merely toothpaste. Thus, the advertisement falsely raises the expectations of the consumer. Such an advertisement can falsely enter into the perception process of the consumer, thus leading to dissatisfaction on the use of the product. Such an advertisement basically confuses people.

Another example of deceptive advertising is the advertisements of beauty products, especially the advertisement of fairness bleaches or fairness creams. They all promise fairness within a certain period of being used. Basically what happens with the use of fairness bleaches is that, the superficial facial hair gets bleached giving an impression of fair skin. Fairness creams on the other hand work at removing the suntan thus getting a clear skin effect. However, the basic ingredient of many fairness soaps and creams is bleach, and bleach is basically harmful for the skin. Research has proved that bleaching also stimulates hair growth, thus leading to more facial hair to be bleached. This effect of bleaching is never revealed in any advertisement of face bleach. The only aspect that is revealed is fairness. But here the relevant question is fairness at what cost? The product does deliver its promise. But is this ethical? Should not a warning be put that bleaching may lead to an increase in facial hair in some cases? But with this warning, would people buy the product? Don't people buy cigarettes despite the warning that cigarette smoking is injurious to health? Thus in the best interest of the consumer, advertisers should portray their products as they are, together with their side effects, and then let the consumers decide whether they want to use them. This is what should ideally happen, but given the competitive situation of our market, until stiff legislation is incorporated to cover every aspect that is harmful for the consumer, the consumer will have to suffer.

Let us take the example of advertisements of various cola-based soft drinks. The advertisements of these products are targeted at people of all ages. Research findings have shown that some of these products are not only harmful for the teeth, but also not good for health in general. The calorie content is high and some of them are also addictive. Do the advertisements of these products ever reveal any of these effects? An advertisement for a product that may have these effects, should it not carry a warning? And if it does not carry a warning, then is it not deceptive? Deceptive advertising takes place when the use of a product even though achieves the result promised in the advertisement, leads to some ill effects, which were not revealed by the advertisement, thus being harmful to the consumer.

2. Forceful Selling

Forceful selling is one of the effects of an improvement in the means of mass communication. Today, every advertiser has to compete severely with other similar and competing products in order to get the consumer to choose his product from amongst a hoard of similar products. Thus, the advertiser is constantly trying to make his product more and more attractive to the prospect. When attractive advertising fails to get the desired response, the advertiser tries to cash in on the human sentiment of getting something for nothing. Thus nowadays most of the advertisements are carriers of sales promotion messages like 'two for the price of one', 'buy two and get one free'.

Another way in which the advertiser forces people to buy is by announcing free gifts on the purchase of the product. Thus, even though the prospect may not have normally bought the product he is lured by the offer of a free gift. An ideal example is the offer by Reader's Digest of a free gift on the purchase of their book on instant medical remedies priced around ₹ 900. Plus they are offering a lucky draw to those prospects who fill in and return the coupons. These coupons have a 'Yes', I want to purchase the book, and 'No', I do not want to purchase the book, but I do not mind going through it without any pressure of buying. The lucky draw has a prize of around one million in gold. Thus, the Readers Digest through this mailer, first and foremost, through the free gift which is offered only to those who place an order, gets people to buy. Secondly, even if they are not lured by the free gift it lures them through the lucky draw coupon through which whether they post the 'yes' coupon or the 'no' coupon the book will be delivered to them. Thus, an obligation to buy is created. This is an ideal example of forceful selling.

Another way in which manufacturers and advertisers resort to forceful selling is by selling images to the people. Thus, the advertisement for a cigarette is not selling a cigarette but a 'macho' image. It is this image that lures people towards the particular product.

Another way in which advertisers are forcing people to buy the products is by cutting into the market of other products. Thus, Cadbury has repositioned its chocolate in such a manner that it replaces the traditional 'mithai' in marriage festivities. Archie's Cards have come up with the celebration of various days and strongly promote these in the media so that, more and more cards get sold. Thus, it creates the occasions, promotes the occasion/event and then sells its products to the consumers.

Another way in which forceful selling is done is by organising exchange 'melas' and off-season discounts. Thus, you will find off-season sales organised for various products so as to get people to buy them in advance. An ideal example of this is an off-season sale of fans in winter and sweaters in the summer. Exchange 'melas' are really rampant with all types of consumer durables. But for these offers, products like televisions and refrigerators would be purchased just once in the lifetime of many an Indian.

Scratch cards, coupons, competitions, dinners with famous personalities are all used to induce the customer to purchase. Most of these competitions are targeted at children through products that are no concern of theirs. Thus, today a child can enter a drawing competition by producing a Surf wrapper. This pressurises mothers into buying Surf. Even if they do not want to, they have to purchase Surf, for the reason that the advertisement itself is targeted at children in such a fashion that, the child will want to enter the competition. Thus, it is advertising through its mass appeal and reach that enables the advertiser to resort to this kind of forceful selling.

3. Media Misuse

Media is that means through which messages reach the masses. These messages have the power not only to influence the actions of the people but they also influence their thinking and their judgements. Not just the youth but also the older generation is privy to being influenced by media, so strong is its impact. Taking into account all these influencing features of media, is it not a misuse of media when products that are potentially dangerous and harmful to life are advertised through this very strong medium? Here the reference is to advertisements of products such as cigarettes, 'pan masala' and alcohol.

Another way in which the media is misused is by showing situations in which young girls and boys behave in a style not socially acceptable in the advertisements. When a particular behaviour is endorsed as acceptable behaviour in the advertisements, it automatically gets reinforced in the minds of the society specially the youth as acceptable behaviour. This leads to a decline in our social values. An ideal example of this is the television advertisement of 'Clinic Plus' in which a young boy upon losing a bet agrees to dance naked amongst a group of boys and girls. Thus an endorsement of this kind of behaviour by advertisements on mass media just puts the stamp of approval on such behaviour, and our easily vulnerable youth is once more influenced towards wrong behaviour. Is this not a misuse of media? There are innumerable such examples of media misuse. Another prominent one that comes to mind is the television advertisement of a pen in the recent past in which a girl kisses a boy because he lends her a pen. This kind of a communication on mass media is sending out a message to the youth that this is acceptable behaviour. But is it? Is this not a misuse of media?

Another way in which media is misused is by our political leaders, in order to carry favour with the masses and project themselves in a right and correct manner. An ideal example of this is the way in which two competing channels in Tamil Nadu reported the arrest of ex-chief minister Karunanidhi. One channel owned and operated by the current chief minister Jayalalitha showed one side of the picture where as the other channel showed a totally contrasting picture. These two kinds of news coverage released by both these channels have created a lot of confusion and speculation in the minds of the people.

Thus the media is a very powerful instrument and if misused can have a very negative impact on society.

4. **Message Problem**

Advertising is a means of mass communication, and communicates with the masses at large. Even in a one-to-one communication process, we face problems. The way in which the message is intended to be delivered and the way in which it is received are different, thus leading to an inefficient communication process. When the communicated message has problems in a two-way, one-to-one communication, then definitely a one-way communication addressed towards a large audience will have problems. Let us study some of these message problems or barriers to the advertising communication.

(i) **Cultural barriers:** India is a vast country with a vast diversity in the cultures of the many people that inhabit it. People of diverse cultural habits inhabit each state and each city. Further the attitudes and perceptions of the people also differ. Thus an advertising communication very acceptable to one set of people may not be acceptable to another set of people. This gives rise to a message problem.

(ii) **Significance of words, symbols, colours etc.:** Certain colours signify something special to a particular sect of people. For example, the saffron colour signifies holiness to the Hindu community where as the same holiness is portrayed by the use of green colour to the Muslim community. The Muslim community holds the numbers 786 in high respect and its use is significant from their point of view. The symbol of the 'swastika' portrays peace for a particular sect of the Indian community. Thus, the use of such colours, symbols and words in the advertising message will give a different meaning to the message depending upon who is receiving it.

(iii) Physical barriers: The message may get distorted leading to a message problem if the receiver of the advertising communication himself suffers from some physical problems like hearing problem, sight problem or a problem of understanding.

The above are some of the barriers that obstruct the delivery of the advertised message in the form in which it was meant to be delivered and understood; thereby creating a message problem.

5. Truth and Advertising

Truth is very important to the sound economic health of the advertising industry. The effectiveness of advertising as a tool of promotion diminishes if the people begin to believe that advertisements are false and cleverly designed to fool them. No advertiser can fool all the consumers all the time. Unfortunately the credibility of advertising has been under criticism for decades and people are of the opinion that advertisements should be more truthful. According to Prof. E. J. Kottman, following are the reasons for the negative opinion of advertising.

(i)   Not all advertisements are truthful. Even a single advertisement containing false statements damages the true image of truthful advertising because human being is a generalising animal – he goes straight to the general from a particular case.

(ii) Most persons – intellectuals and critics alike – do not make a difference between factual statements and value judgements.

(iii) The meanings which people ascribe to advertisements, are frequently different from those stated or implied, in other words people infer notions or formulate their own propositions that are untrue or unbelievable and conclude that it is the advertising that is untrue.

(iv) Each advertisement appears to be full of contradictions stated, implied or inferred. Thus, each producer says 'his product is the best'. In fact, it cannot be; this makes the consumers take all such advertisements at a discount.

(v)   Many advertisements focus on the trivial, particularly the nationwide advertisements of products such as soft drinks, cosmetics, soaps, drugs etc. It attempts to make the insignificant seem significant, and in so doing, earns for advertising a kind of pseudo image.

Truly speaking it is not easy to define the term 'truth' as it is the most elusive term. Right from times immemorial, the entire world is in search of truth; yet no one knows about its nature and whereabouts. It is the greatest philosophical controversy. However, for an average human being truth means facts, things as they have happened or taken place over a period of time. For the common man truth is the same as judicial truth. Judicial truth is the content of the 'swear' taken by each person upon entering the witness box. Here, truth means the 'whole of the facts as they have taken place without any mixing of lies with the facts'.

The judicial truth is not applicable to the world of advertising. That is why no advertisement gives the demerits of the product or service. It paints a rosy picture of the brighter side only. The truth of advertising is not the judicial truth, but the commercial truth. Advertising would be respected even if it just delivered the commercial truth. But the main drawback of advertising is that so many times even the commercial truth is not there. In our daily advertisements, we come across untruth in varying degrees. The different forms of untruths in advertising are as under:

(i) **Exaggerated facts:** Majority of advertisers make very tall claims about their products and services. There is some truth in their claims. However, it is too magnified to be believable. For example claims of ready-made garments manufacturers, saying that the pant crease will remain fresh all day long; their garments require no ironing; or will not fade. The claim of soap and fairness cream manufacturers that their soap will lead to a clear complexion; the cream will lead to fair and clear skin; or the claim of shampoo manufacturers to healthy hair in just 14 days. All these claims though have a certain element of truth; do not result in exactly the promised effect. Thus, truth prevails but at an inflated rate.

(ii) **Misrepresentation of facts:** So many times advertisers misrepresent the facts in such a way so as to mislead the audience into believing something that does not exist. For example, the label of export quality; this label is put in order to mislead the public into believing that the product was intended for exports. However, export quality is just a label for home made goods, not actually meant for exports.

(iii) **Unverifiable claims in a language that is ambiguous:** Advertisements of energy drinks like 'Complan' and 'Boost' talk about how one glass can give you all the energy or about it being the complete health food. For example *Boost is the secret of my energy* or *Complan the complete health food*. What is the meaning of health food? Does just drinking Complan keep you healthy? Does Boost really give you energy? Such unverifiable claims are the stuff of today's slick advertising. The advertisements for baby food like Cerelac and Farex make similar claims. So do biscuits and cereal chocolates nowadays.

(iv) **The use of testimonials or endorsements:** Advertisers pay handsome fees to film and sports personalities who have nothing to do with the use of the product or service, to endorse their products. For example, Kapil Dev promoted Boost, a range of film actresses promoted Lux, but the crown goes to Sachin Tendulkar who, as reported in the press, has been offered a contract for a period of 5 years with World Tel to promote products only for them.

(v) **The use of sex, specially the use of women as sex objects to advertise:** Products that are targeted at men—products such as cars, motorcycles, two wheelers, aftershave lotions and even underwear ads frequently show a scantily clad woman in western garments. In fact, the height of this is the ad for the soft drink Sprite that shows a model soaked in a bathtub full of the soft drink.

(vi) **Alcohol and tobacco advertisements:** All tobacco advertisements show that macho men smoke. Such ads also talk of brave deeds being done by smokers. There is no relationship between bravery and smoking, but the advertisements are made in such a way that it misleads one into believing that smoking and bravery go hand in hand. Similarly most alcohol advertisements show alcohol as friendship. The McDowell ad that features Dharmendra gives the viewer the impression that McDowell's Whiskey is the binding factor between Dharmendra and the common man, thus misleading the public.

(vii) **Totally false claims:** Many times, advertisers make statements that have virtually no truth in them at all. A good many advertisements give false statistics, fake certificates and testimonials of famous people with captions like *'millions cannot go wrong'*, *'believe it or not', 'strange but true'*, are only a few examples of this kind. Further, advertisements that offer freedom and independence make blatantly false claims.

All these forms of untruthful advertisements prevail because the consumers have neither the time nor the power to discover such cheats. Basically, they are unorganised. Such practices will continue so long as the consumers will tolerate them.

In conclusion, it can be said that the advertiser has a moral and social responsibility and cannot afford to indulge in malpractices that affect interest. He cannot afford to go astray because:

- His reputation is at stake.
- He cannot take undue advantage of the trust or the faith that the consumers have put in advertising.
- He has a legal responsibility.
- The consumers are getting organised and becoming aware of such acts.
- Truth never fails.

An advertiser cannot fool all the people all the time. In short, it pays the advertiser to be honest in stating to his consumers, what his goods and services are, what they do and how effectively.

6. Life Styles and Values: Moral Influences

Advertising by its very nature receives wide coverage. Furthermore, it presumably has an effect on what people buy and thus on their activities. Because of this coverage and its role as a persuasive vehicle, it is argued that it has an impact on the values and lifestyles of society.

Here, the pertinent question that needs our attention is – In what way does advertising affect the cultural values and lifestyle of a nation or society? In order to have a better understanding of this question, let us divide it into three parts; namely, Is advertising a product of culture? Does advertising shape the cultural values of society? Are the cultural values reflected always in advertising?

(A) Is Advertising a Product of Culture?

The answer is definitely "yes". This is because advertising is subservient to the society and its needs. The culture of a society is not the product of advertising. Advertising as a social and economic institution, is a servant and not the master of consumers. In fact, advertising is the product of culture. Advertising has the power to persuade people to buy products and services. However, this does not mean that advertising can persuade the consumer to buy anything under the sun, even if he does not want, need and desire it, just because it is advertised. Today, we know that, we buy only those goods and services that we need, and we want, based on social values having a cultural tinge.

An individual learns the attitudes, values, norms of conduct acceptable to the cultural group in the formative years of his life. The major forces that train him in cultural norms and values are his family, school, college, church or temple and social contacts. These cultural values are the basis for selecting and evaluating goods and services. Individual buying behaviour is the result of the sociological environment of people of which cultural values is the base. His social class, family status, family life cycle, social relations, reference groups, opinion leaders and life style influence his behaviour.

However, the value system that has been developed is not static. In fact it is ever changing. With these changes in values, the role of advertising and its theme also changes to keep pace with the changing times. In the past, Indian society and Indian culture stressed 'spiritual' living. That is why everyone in the society earned just enough to meet his minimum and simple needs. As wants were limited there was contentment amongst the people. Today however, the value system has changed totally. We are more materialistic and hence the philosophy is to earn more and enjoy more. Today is important! Yesterday has gone, and tomorrow may never come. What is certain is only now. Hence the advertising message will also reveal such a mentality of the people. It has to, in order to appeal to the people. In effect advertising changes itself so as to uphold the changing philosophy, ideals, beliefs, attitudes, likes and dislikes that the society holds.

Does Advertising Shape the Cultural Values of Society?

No it definitely does not. Once a particular set of values have been imbibed, accepted and continued by society, advertising as a social and business process tries to bring all those goods and services that are made to respect the prevailing value system.

As the current philosophy of modern life is hedonistic, advertising will pass on the same message through refined goods and services, so that the consumer can enjoy the cream of life. Advertising through its persuasive role makes people so aware of the available products, that yesterday's comforts become today's necessities. Thus, everyone will be after what is latest. Be it toothpaste, a soft or hot drink, automobiles, housing or medical care. Such refinements expected and respected by the consumer, makes advertising create a demand for newer goods, resulting in increased production, economies of scale, more employment, more earnings, more demand and therefore more production in turn. Thus, the cycle of wants, efforts and satisfaction completes the emphasis on a refined or quality life.

In precise terms advertising becomes a major wheel in the mechanism of production and distribution. It refines the quality of life within the limits set by the value system of society. Advertising cannot shape the original needs and wants. It only gives the finishing touches so as to refine the original demand within the broad limits set by the values of society. Advertising has the role of creating, and cultivating demand, and striving to make the goods and services available so as to satisfy the customer to the maximum extent possible.

Are Cultural values always reflected in Advertising?

The answer to this question is certainly 'no'. It is not always that we see advertising absorbing all the cultural values of society. Many times, it is against the esteemed values or norms of an acceptable culture. The problem of today's society is how to do away with ill effects of drinking, smoking, gambling, prostitution and drug addiction. These happenings in the world of today go to show that advertising does not have total cultural control.

Advertising is doing its work of persuasion that is, converting desire into demand without bothering must about the good or ill effects of the goods and services that it brings to the notice of the consumers. Thus, a cigarette manufacturer speaks very highly of his brand as the best. State governments speak of lotteries to make a few million every month or every week. Liquor producers are promising seventh heavens to the consumer. All of us know that these have a disastrous and degenerating effect on the physical and mental health of the people. Advertising does not care for this degeneration, as it does not discourage these products. It is neutral or mild in this regard. Only a statutory warning is not enough to do away with these ill effects on society and culture. Advertising should uphold the cultural values that we have learnt in our families, schools, colleges, churches and temples, in our friend circles, in the contacts with those who are near and far to us.

However, we can conclude by saying that advertising does reflect the values of society. However, if a product is harmful to society and outside its cultural bounds, but there is scope of making money through its production and sale, not only do producers promote such products, but in some instances the government too allows them. Saying that advertising affects values, is not totally true as advertising does not have the power to dominate other forces such as family, religion, literature and so on that contribute to the values of society.

1.2 Strategic Advertising Decisions

1.2.1 Setting Advertising Objectives

The objectives of advertising are derived from the marketing objectives of the company, which, in turn, are derived from the overall corporate objectives. Here, let us understand the difference between advertising objectives and goals. An objective is a broad aim where as a goal is a specific quantified task. Often, advertising objectives in the marketing plans are vaguely worded in general, terms, such as, 'to increase sales and profits', 'to expand our share of the market', or 'to maintain a favourable attitude towards our company among the trade and consuming public'. Evaluation of these objectives is basically not possible because there are no criteria for evaluation. Further, a lack of clarity in setting advertising objectives may arise due to the following reasons:

- Problem in stating objectives in quantifiable terms.
- Apparent failure in realising that the results of advertising cannot be generally measured in terms of sales.
- Inability in identifying the target audience.
- Inadequate information about media, its qualitative focus and reach.

The examples of objectives of advertising that are given above are basically marketing objectives. To increase the market share is a marketing objective. Advertising objectives should be stated only in terms of communication. Advertising can give added value to a brand by appealing to the consumers' reasoning, his senses and his emotions. It cannot affect direct sales, as sales depend not only on advertising but on a number of other variables of the marketing mix. Advertising is just one element of the promotion mix of the company. It works together with other elements like personal selling, retailer recommendations, publicity, special promotions, and the like. Thus, even the achievement of the communication objective does not depend upon advertising alone, as advertising is used in combination with other elements of the promotion mix of the company.

Thus, advertising objectives in order to be valid should actually be made out as specific communication objectives. As broad objectives are difficult to quantify and measure, what are used are advertising goals or tasks. The ideal advertising goal should be stated as a specific communication task to be accomplished among a defined audience to a given degree in a given period of time. Further, it should be usable as a measure to evaluate the effectiveness of the advertisements. The following are some examples of quantifiable advertising goals:

1. To ensure that a particular advertising message, "Now Gillette blade gives 5 extra shaves per blade" reaches 10 million people of the target audience.

2. To increase awareness by 20% among the target group about the following: "The cleaning action of Surf Ultra is the best and it washes whitest of all".

3. To communicate to all existing purchasers that a particular brand has improved because the product is now sealed in a new airtight container to maintain freshness and aroma.

Once the advertising goals are set, they should be written down and all parties who are involved in making decisions on advertising should agree to them. This not only helps in the creation of the advertisement, end the advertising campaign, but cuts down waste as everyone has the same goals in mind. Once the basic approach is agreed upon, plans should be drawn up to reach the goals. Next, a price tag should be given to each task that is necessary to achieve the goals. Then, according to its priority rating, a cost analysis of the entire operation should then be made and an advertising budget must be prepared. In the final stage, the creative and media plans should be worked out.

1.2.2 Deciding Advertising Budget

Advertising is a very powerful tool of mass communication. It is also a highly expensive one. Not only commercial business houses but also the government and social organisations find advertising to be a very useful tool in achieving their marketing goals and objectives. Even though advertising is very expensive and millions of rupees are spent on advertising, yet we find that the decisions on advertising expenditure are often taken in an arbitrary manner and, sometimes, even based on intuition and guesswork.

An organisation, in order to achieve the desired goals has to take the help of advertising. Proper advertising desires that the right media be selected. Selection of media depends upon the funds available for advertising, as a major part of the advertising budget is spent on purchasing time and space in media. Also, for the advertising to be effective, the right time and right space is to be purchased. All this depends upon the finance available for advertising. Sometimes, it so happens that there is a gross inadequacy of funds for advertising and, at times, there is a wanton extravagance. In order that such an imbalanced situation does not occur, what is required is to see that proper planning is done for advertising expenditure. In other words, advertising expenditure requires good planning. Budgeting is a form of plan and, in the very nature of budgeting, the advertiser is protected from a situation in which too much or too less is available for advertising expenditure. While preparing the advertising budget, the advertiser has to consider how much he will be spending on each product or on each product line, on each of his markets, on each media, and on what time schedule during the year.

Budget a Plan

The advertising budget is a plan of the company's future advertising. It provides a programme of the various available types of advertising to be undertaken in the future together with the timetable and frequency. Today, what is required is a planned advertising expenditure as advertising is very essential to build up a consumer franchise for a particular brand. It should be very clear as to when, where and to what extent advertising is to be done. An advertising plan (budget) makes these points very clear.

In addition to its planning function, the budget also acts as a controlling factor on advertising expenditure. Because of the advertising budget, the expenditure on advertising is kept within certain specified boundaries. Today, expenditure on advertising is not considered an expenditure but an investment, because of the greater returns that are expected in future because of the increase in sales due to advertising. In the words of David Oligvy, the pundit of modern advertising, "Every advertisement is a long-term investment in the image of a brand".

Steps in Advertising Budget Making Process / Advertising Budget Procedure

The budget procedure or the budgetary process is made up of four logical steps as under:

1. Budget preparation

The first step in the budgetary process is the preparation of the budget. The preparation of the budget requires time and brains on the part of the advertising department. Generally, the advertising budget is planned and designed by the advertising manager with the help and assistance of his staff as well as the personnel of the advertising agency. The company's marketing plan which gives detailed information about the company's markets, sales, distribution, competition, and the like is used as a base for preparing the advertising budget. This budget is to be prepared using suitable method or methods of appropriation. The total advertising budget so prepared is to be divided amongst various heads of expenditure. These figures of the total budget as well as the budgeted figures of the various heads of expenditure should be realistic.

2. Budget presentation

The budget thus prepared is to be presented to the higher ups for approval. The presentation of the budget to the top management is a sales job and requires a lot of skills on the part of the advertising manager. He has to convince the top management, which is not only a watchdog, on the expenditure but also one that holds the strings to the finance. They are there to keep a check on any wasteful expenditure. Thus, in getting the budget approved, the advertising manager has to convince the top management about the essentiality of each item of expenditure on the advertising budget. Even though getting the budget approved is the job of the advertising manager, the advertising agency provides the necessary visual material and the moral support.

3. Budget implementation

Once the budget is approved, the funds are available at the command of the advertising manager, and he is responsible for their spending as per the budget. The advertising manager basically appoints an advertising agency, and the agency, in turn, buys the time and space in media. Even though buying time and space in media is the agency's responsibility, the advertising manager has to keep a check to see that the agency is prudent in their spending. He has to prepare a proper procedure for placing orders, delegating the authority to buy and to verify and approve before making the final payment. This is because in the absence of such set procedures, the company may not get the best discounts thereby resulting in waste of scare resources. It is this vigilance on his part that saves the finances of his company, and keeps him ahead of his competitors.

4. Budget control

Once the advertising budget is implemented, the next logical step is to check whether it has been implemented as per plan. This step of checking is known as budget control. Budget control has three phases, namely, expenditure control, commitment control and management control.

Expenditure control is the control on the actual approval and payment of invoices for the ad materials and services. In addition to the money spent, much more is usually committed well before the receipts and invoices are received and such commitments emerge mainly from approved media schedules and cost of preparing jobs in production. Thus 'commitment control' enables the manager to match his actual expenditure with the committed one, to know the overall situation. 'Management control' is an occasional review of the advertising efforts in terms of results. Thus, the entire exercise of budget process ends with a check on the various aspects of expenditure and the result or effect of advertising. If the expenditure was within the bounds set by the budget and has resulted in the desired results, the budget exercise is said to be executed as per plan.

1.2.3 Advertising Framework: Planning and Organising

Advertising strategy specifically means the art of planning operations so as to ensure results. In more simple terms we can say that an advertiser in this competitive era coupled with marketing challenges and complex changes cannot blindly venture into any promotion or advertising campaign without planning and organising his advertising strategies.

In the process of formulating his advertising strategy he should primarily enter in the process of planning operations strategically. He could very well begin with the building of planning premises, organisation and effectiveness and channelise it with effective contribution towards the attainment of the advertising features layout during the various short-term, medium-term or long-term promotion programmes or advertising campaign of the organisation.

Planning and Organisation Contribution

Planning, as we all are aware, is a preparatory management step for action. It refers to a systematised pre-thinking for determining a definite course of action to achieve some derived result. While formulating any advertising strategy the elements, aspects and all essentials of planning should be considered.

Organisation is also an important function of management. It is both a foundation as well as a tool of efficient management. It is a framework within which people can work in co-operation and through which management can get things done effectively. In the area of advertising and especially when we are talking in terms of advertising strategy, the organisation aspect becomes more relevant and significant as it deals or refers to the management in which the channel of communication pattern of influence and lines of authority are structured in a business enterprise. If the inward communication process or system is sound, then naturally the outward communication, that is, advertisement will also be sound and effective.

In the study of advertising strategy the contribution aspect is also very significant. The contribution refers to the co-ordination, assistance and support of each planned advertising strategy. Contribution thus refers to the integration and blending of each advertising activity such as advertising decisions, media strategy, market segment strategy how these work in fusion and help in attaining the advertising directives.

Setting of advertising objectives

The pivotal aspect of any advertising management effort is the development of meaningful objectives. Without good objectives, it is nearly impossible to guide and control decision-making. Good performance may occasionally occur in the absence of objectives, but it can rarely be sustained. In the past, advertising had often been a free spirit without an organisation operating with little guidance or control. It has been able to resist the discipline of modern management because the actual creative decision was usually made in another organisation, the advertising agency. The challenge today is to bring effective management to the advertising process in such a way so as to provide stimulation as well as direction to be creative effort. The key therefore is the development of meaningful aspects or defining advertising goals for measured results. A study of this is very crucial for all who deal with advertising.

Defining Advertising Goals for Measured Advertising results (DAGMAR)

In 1961, Russel H. Collet wrote a book called Defining Advertising Goal for Measured Advertising Results. The book introduced what has become known as the DAGMAR approval to advertising play.

The DAGMAR approval can be summarised into succinct statement defining an advertising goal or an advertising objective.

An advertising goal is a specific communicating task to be accomplished among a defined audience, on a given period of time. The goal is specific involving definite task, in a required given period. To understand the DAGMAR approval it is very essential to study what a communication task or goal is, and what a specific task or objective is.

A Communication Task

An advertising objective involves a communication task, something that advertising, by itself, can reasonably hope to accomplish. It is recognised that advertising is mass, paid communication that is intended to create awareness, impart information, develop attitudes or induce action.

In DAGMAR, the communication task is based on a specific model or the communication process. The model suggests that there is a series of mental steps through which a brand or object must climb to gain acceptance. An individual starts at some point by being unaware of the brand's presence in the market. The initial task of the brand is to gain awareness to advance one step up the hierarchy.

The second step of brand comprehension involves the audience member learning something about the brand. What are its special characteristics and appeals? In what way does it differ from its competition? Whom is it supposed to benefit? The third step is the attitude (or conviction) step and intervenes between comprehension and final action. The action phase involves some over move on the part of the buyer like trying a brand for the first time, visiting a showroom, or requesting information.

A communication model like the DAGMAR model with the implication that the audience member will sequentially pass through a set of steps is termed a "hierarchy-of-effects" model. A host of hierarchy models have been proposed. The AIDA model, developed in the 1920s suggested that effective personal sales presentation should attract attention, gain interact, create a desire, and precipitate action. The new adopter hierarchy may be conceived by rural sociologists, postulated five stages: awareness, interaction, evaluation, trial, and adoption.

Another hierarchy model is particularly interesting because of its ties with social psychological theory. Developed by Robert Lavidge and Steiner, it includes six stages: awareness, knowledge, liking, preference, conviction, and purchase. They divided this hierarchy into components corresponding to a social psychologist's concept of an attend system. The first stage, consisting of the awareness and knowledge levels, is comparable to the cognitive or knowledge component of attitude. The affective components of an attitude, the like-dislike aspect, are represented in the Lavidge and Steiner hierarchy by the liking and preference levels. The remaining attitude component in the cognitive component, the action or motivation element, represented by the conviction and purchase levels, are the final two levels in the hierarchy.

A Specific Task

We have mentioned that DAGMAR emphasises the communication task of advertising as contrasted to the marketing objectives of the firm. The second important concept of DAGMAR is that the advertising goal be specific. It should be a written measurable task involving a starting point, a defined audience, and a fixed time period.

Measurable

DAGMAR needs to be made specific when actual goals are formulated. When brand comprehension is involved, for example, it is necessary to indicate exactly what appeal or image is to be communicated. Furthermore, the specification should include a description of the measurement procedure. If a high-protein cereal were trying to gain brand comprehension, managers could well decide to promote its protein content. However, merely mentioning its protein content is inadequate and open to different interpretations. Is the cereal to be perceived as one containing a full-day's supply as a protection against illness or as one that supplies more energy than other cereals? If a survey includes the request 'rank the following cereals as to protein content', then brand comprehension could be quantified to mean the percentage who rated it first.

Benchmark

President Lincoln has been quoted as saying, "If we could first know where we are and where we are tending, we could better judge what to do and how to do it". A basic aspect of establishing a goal or selecting a campaign to reach it is to know the starting conditions. Without a benchmark, it is most difficult to determine the optimal goal. The selection of an awareness-oriented goal might be a mistake if awareness is already high. Without a benchmark measure, such a circumstance could not be ascertained quantitatively. In addition, benchmarks can suggest how a certain goal can best be reached. For example, it would be useful to know whether the existing image needs to be changed, reinforced, or sharpened. A benchmark is also a pre-requisite to the ultimate measurement of results and essential part of any planning programme and of DAGMAR in particular. Despite the obvious value of having benchmarks before goals are set this is often not done. In fact, the key to DAGMAR is probably the generation of well-conceived benchmarks before advertising goals are determined. With such measures, the rest of the approach flows rather naturally.

The Target

A key tenet of DAGMAR was that the target audience be well-defined. If the goal was to increase awareness among the heavy user segment from 25% to 60% in a certain time period, the benchmark measures could not be developed without a specification of the target segment. Further, the campaign execution will normally depend on the identity of the target segment. The heavy user group will likely respond differently from a segment defined by a lifestyle profile.

Time Period

The objective should involve a particular time period, such as six months or one year. With a time period specified, a survey to generate a set of measures can be planned and anticipated. All parties involved will understand that the results will be available for evaluating the campaign which could lead to a contraction, expansion, or change in the current effort. The length of the time period must fit into various constraints involving the planning cycle of both a company and an agency. However, the appropriate time necessary to generate the kind of cognitive responsibility desired should also be considered.

Written

Finally, goals should be committed to paper. Under the discipline of writing clearly, basic shortcomings and misunderstandings become exposed and it becomes easy to determine whether the goal contains the crucial aspects of the DAGMAR approach.

Suppose that the product of interest were an economy-priced bourbon, it has a bad quality image despite the fact that blind taste tests indicated that it does not have any real quality problems. An objective might be developed with respect to a scale ranging from – 5 to + 5 (inadequate taste to adequate taste). An admissible objective would be to increase the percentage of male bourbon drinkers in the United States who give a non-negative rating on the scale from 5 to 25 percent in a 12-month period. Notice that, this objective is measurable, has a starting point, a definite audience, and a fixed time period.

Implementation – The 6M Approach

The DAGMAR book was not very specific in its advice to the person charged with its implementation. It did, however, provide guidelines that gave additional insight into its basic philosophy. One suggestion was that a systematic information gathering process, termed the 6M approach, be employed to analyse the market and product situation. The objective was to stimulate ideas or decision alternatives, thus guiding the manager toward more optimal decisions. The 6M approach is structured around six categories of analysis: merchandise, markets, motives, messages, media, and measurements.

Merchandise – Product Strategy

This suggests an evaluation of the relative strengths and weaknesses of the product. What are the benefits offered by the product and how do they compare with those offered by the competition? Do any of these benefits stand out as significant contributors to the product's differential advantage?

Markets – Market Segmentation Strategy

This involves the present and the intermediaries distributing it. One objective is to identify alternative segmentation strategies. As the preceding discussion suggested, many types of segmentation variables can be considered. Basic statistics covering the size and characteristics of the market usually provide a starting place. Consumption habits and buying influences are among the other variables that are usually introduced. A second consideration is intermediaries – the components of the distribution channel. The effect of advertising on distributors, wholesalers, and retailers is often overlooked. However, advertising has an important role to play for many products in influencing intermediaries. Basic questions should be asked. For example, what are the critical factors in sales growth? Are some associated with the trade? If so, what should advertising's role be?

Motives – Consumer Behaviour Strategy, Pricing Strategy

Why do people buy? What rational and emotional reasons underlie purchase decision? What motives are involved? What are the relevant consumption systems within which the product is embedded? What are the goals of these consumption systems? The concept of the consumption system is often a useful device to gain understanding. When it is realised that orange juice is used not only at large and small breakfasts, but also with snacks, at cocktail parties, and so on, a feel is obtained for the heterogeneity of consumer motives. The goals of a breakfast are far different from those of a cocktail party, and the wants and needs of the consumer are also different.

Message

What alternative appeals could influence prospective consumers to purchase? What appeals have been used in the past by our products and by the competition? There is usually some value in being different and it is essential to avoid being so similar to a previous competitor's advertisement that the appeal is transferred by the reader to the competitor's brand. For example, some automobile advertising benefits from similar competitor's advertising.

Media – Promotion Strategy

This refers to the media decisions and constraints that are involved. They can interact meaningfully with the segment selected and the appearance used.

Measurement – Advertising Strategy

This refers to the measures that need to be obtained during this audit stage, not only to provide benchmarks to measure future progress, but also to provide real guidance in establishing objectives.

THE DAGMAR CHECKLIST

Another aid to those implementing the Dagmar approach is a checklist of promotional tasks.

The suggestion was to rate each of the promotional tasks in terms of its relative importance in the context of the product situation involved. Again, the intent was to stimulate ideas or decision alternatives, often the most difficult and crucial part of the decision process.

Following are two examples of the DAGMAR approach as presented in Colley's book. It is left to the reader to examine these examples critically to see if they satisfy the requirements of the approach as it has been presented here.

Partial Checklist of Promotional Tasks

To what extent does the advertising aim at closing an immediate sale?

1. Perform the complete selling function (take the product through all the necessary steps towards a sale).
2. Close sales to prospects already partly sold through past advertising efforts ("ask for the order" for "clincher" advertising).
3. Announce a special reason for "buying now" (price, premium etc.).
4. Remind people to buy.
5. Tie-in with some special buying event.
6. Stimulate impulse sales. Does the advertising aim at near-term sales by moving the prospect, step by step, closer to a sale (so that when confronted with a buying situation the customer will ask for, reach for, or accept the advertised brand)?
7. Create awareness of existence of the product or brand.
8. Create brand image or favourable emotional disposition toward the brand.
9. Implant information or attitude regarding benefits and superior features of brand.
10. Combat or offset competitive claims.
11. Correct false impressions, misinformation, and other obstacles to sales.
12. Build familiarity and easy recognition of package or trademark. Does the advertising aim at building a long-range consumer franchise?
13. Build confidence in company and brand, which is expected to pay in years to come.
14. Build customer demand that places the company in a stronger position in relation to its distribution (not at the "mercy of the marketplace").
15. Place advertiser in a position to select preferred distributors and dealers.
16. Secure universal distribution.
17. Establish a "reputation platform" for launching new brands of product lines.
18. Establish brand recognition and acceptance that will enable the company to open up new markets (geographic, price, age, sex). How important are supplementary benefits of end-use advertising?
19. Aid sales people in opening new accounts.
20. Aid sales people in getting larger orders from wholesalers and retailers.
21. Aid sales people in getting preferred display space.
22. Give sales people an entry.
23. Build morale of company sales force.
24. Impress the trade.

CHALLENGES TO DAGMAR

DAGMAR had enormous visibility and influence. It really changed the way that advertising objectives were created and the way that advertising results were measured. It introduced the concept of communication objectives like awareness, comprehension, image and attitude. The point was made that such goals are more appropriate for advertising than some measure like sales which can have multiple causes. In introducing communication objectives, behavioural science constructs and models such as attitude models were drawn upon. DAGMAR also focused attention upon measurement encouraging people to create objectives so specific and operational that they can be measured. In doing so, it provided the potential to improve the communication between the creative teams and the advertising clients.

A measure of the significance of an idea is the degree of both theoretical and empirical controversy that it precipitates. By this measure DAGMAR has been most significant. There have been six different kinds of challenges to DAGMAR.

Sales Goal

First, some purists believe that only a sales measure is relevant. As pointed out by Michael Halbert, one of the pioneers at DuPont, engaged in the use of experimental design approaches to measure advertising effect.

He says, "When a study using one of the goals just mentioned (for example, increase awareness) is published and reported at a meeting, I sometimes get the unsocial urge to question the author with, 'So What?'. If he has shown that advertising does, in fact, increase brand name awareness or favourable attitude toward the company, on what grounds does this increase a justifiable use of the company's funds? The answer usually given is that more people will buy a product if they are aware of it or if they have a favourable attitude. But why leave this critical piece of inference out of the design of the original research?"

"For example, if awareness does not affect sales, why bother to measure it? If it does have a close relationship, why not measure sales directly? This is not the place to review the relevant arguments. Suffice it to say that there is a disagreement and that a more refined model of the communication process than is now available must eventually evolve."

Practicability

A second objection focuses on the many implementation difficulties inherent in the DAGMAR approach. In particular, the 6M approach and the checklist fall short of providing sufficient details to implement the approach. As Leo Bogart has observed, "Colley provides broad outlines much like the dragonfly that, after showing a hippopotamus the relationship between wing movement and flying, was asked exactly how to do it and replied, I'll give you the broad idea and you work out the details." A level in the hierarchy to be attacked must be selected, and a campaign to influence those at that level must be developed. Neither of these tasks is easy.

Measurement Problems

The third problem is measurement. What should we really measure when we speak of attitude, awareness or brand comprehension? Substantial conceptual and measurement problems underlie all these constructs.

Noise in the System

A fourth problem is noise that exists in the hierarchy model, just as it does in the other, simpler, response models involving in immediate sales. We have argued that there are many casual factors other than advertising that determine sales. In a more complex model, it can be argued that there are many casual factors besides advertising that determine awareness. For example, variables such as competitive promotion of unplanned publicity can affect an awareness campaign.

Inhibiting the Great Idea

The "great creative idea" is a dream, or hope of many advertisers. DAGMAR is basically a rational, planned approach that, among other things, provides guidance to creative people. The problem is that if it does in fact have any influence on their work, it must first necessarily inhibit their efforts. When the creative approach of copywriters and art directors is inhibited, there is less likelihood that they will come up with a great idea and an increased probability of a pedestrian advertising campaign resulting. Of course, there might also be a lesser probability of a spectacularly ineffective advertising campaign.

Anthony Morgan, an agency research director, argues that the hierarchy model, which he terms the 'HEAR-UNDERSTAND-DO' model, inhibits great advertising by emphasising tests of recall, communication and persuasion. He gives two examples. First, a campaign with all music and warm human visuals which everyone loved failed to meet the "company standard" for the day-after-recall test (where on the day after ad exposure, viewers are asked to recall specific copy points). A potentially great campaign was clearly being evaluated by the wrong criteria. A more appropriate model for this campaign might have been "SENSE-FEEL-RELATE".

The second example is the Campbell soup: "Soup is Good Food" campaign created to arrest a 10-year decline in per capital consumption of their Red & White line of soups. The campaign objectives were to communicate news, to change the perception of soup, and to increase consumption. The first commercials received the lowest persuasion scores (from a test measuring the impact of commercial exposure on attitudes and intentions) than any Campbell's commercial had ever scored. However, the campaign, which stimulated three years of sales increases, was designed not to have much initial impact but to withstand enormous repetitions and to work overtime. The testing was simply inappropriate. The implication is that it can be dangerous to rely on testing based on the hierarchical model (or any other single conceptualisation). Rather, conceptual and research flexibility needs to be employed.

Hierarchy Model of Communication Effect

The sixth type of argument against the DAGMAR approach attacks the basic hierarchy model which postulates a set of sequential steps of awareness, comprehension, and attitude leading to action. The counter argument is that other models may be sold in various contexts and that it is naive to apply the DAGMAR hierarchy models in all situations. For example, action can precede attitude formation and even comprehension with an impulse purchase of a low involvement product. At this point there is general agreement that, indeed, the appropriate model will depend upon the situation and a key problem in many contexts is in fact to determine what that model is. However, the basic thrust of DAGMAR, the use of advertising response measures as the basis of objectives and the focus on measurement, does not depend upon the DAGMAR hierarchy model so the issue is not really that social as may have once appeared.

Advertising Strategy

As already discussed earlier an advertising strategy is the group of planned operations, to bring out effective results.

In the field of advertising the following are the important advertising strategies:

1. Segmentation strategy
2. Positive strategy
3. Media strategy/Message strategy
4. Market mix strategy

The advertiser should develop specific strategies and tactics by keeping in view the following aspects:

1. Consumer behaviour and motives
2. Innovative and creative messages, appeals, and copy
3. Media planning, Media mix, Media channels, Media scheduling, Media budget
4. Competitive aspects and approaches
5. Stimulating information
6. Brand positioning
7. Market separation factors
8. The price quality approach
9. The use or application approach
10. The product user approach
11. The product class approach
12. The cultural and social aspects
13. Distribution aspects
14. Packaging
15. Government laws and rules etc.

ADVERTISEMENT PLANNING – LEVEL OF DECISION-MAKING – ADVERTISEMENT SITUATION

In the study of advertising, management planning and decision-making are very much integrated and co-related and they are all focused at a situation. As a matter of fact viewing the marketing environment and thus making the structural analysis effective advertising plans can emerge to be executed so that at various levels decision-making can be done. Hence, we will not study these three topics in isolation but simultaneously.

Advertising Planning and Decision-making

The major activities of advertising management are basically planning and decision-making. In most instances the advertising manager will be involved in the development, implementation and overall management of an advertising plan. The development of an advertising plan essentially requires the generation and specification of alternatives. The alternatives can be various levels of expenditure, different kinds of objectives or strategy possibilities and numerous kinds of options associated with copy creation and media choices. The essence of planning is thus to find out what the feasible alternatives are, and reduce them to a set on which decision can be made.

Levels of Decision-making

Decision-making involves choosing among the alternatives. A complete advertising strategy as stated earlier truly reflects the end result of the planning and decision-making process and the decisions that have been arrived at in a particular product and market situation.

The planning and decision-making process begins with a thorough analysis of the situation facing the advertising as already explained in this chapter earlier.

This step is often caused as the situational analysis used to reflect the fact that situation must be well understood before one special and decision-oriented various levels.

ADVERTISEMENT SITUATION/SITUATION ANALYSIS

The planning and decision-making process begins with a thorough analysis of the situation facing the advertiser. Situation analysis or advertising situation involves an analysis of all important factors operating in a particular given situation. In many cases this means that new research and advanced studies will be undertaken as well as relying on company history and experience.

AT&T for example developed a new strategy for its long-distance telephone services based on five years of research studies.

The research encompassed market segmentation studies, concept testing and large scale field experiment. The field experiment focused on testing a new advertising campaign called "cost of visit". An existing "reach out" campaign, although successful, did not appear to get through to a large group of people who had reasons to call but were limiting their calls because of cost. Research based on annual survey of 3,000 residential telephone users showed that most did not know the cost of a long-distance call or that it was possible to make less expensive calls in off-peak periods. Five copy alternatives were subsequently developed and tested from which "cost of visit" was chosen. The campaign was credited with persuading customers to call during times that were both cheaper for them and more profitable for AT&T and overall, was more effective than the "reach out" campaign. One estimate was that by switching $30 million in advertising from "reach out" to "cost of visit" an incremental gain in revenue of $22 million would result in the first year, and would top $100 million over five years.

This example highlights a "situation" in which advertising was undoubtedly a major factor, extensive research was done to study the situation, and large sums of money were involved in both research and advertising. A complete research analysis will cover all marketing components and involve finding answers to dozens of questions about the nature and extent of demand, competition, environmental factors, products, costs, distribution and the skills and financial resources of the firm.

Situation analysis invariably involves research of some kind. For advertising planning and decision-making, the principal thrust of research efforts will be on market analysis or more broadly, the analysis of consumer motivation and behaviour with respect to the product, service idea or object to be advertised and many of the research approaches techniques, models and results presented throughout this subject pertain to it. Many people in advertising are sceptical about the value of research, particularly with respect to the creative process of actually generating specific advertisement. Although research can slow down the process and some would argue can interfere with creativity, can lead to mundane advertising. In most cases planning and decision-making will be improved by research. Situation analysis can be based on conventional wisdom, managerial experience, or the creative team's inherent imaginative abilities, but current market and environmental condition – what the situation is now – can only be adequately assessed by research. Such research flows from the company and its agency's research efforts, secondary data sources, and/or is purchased from research suppliers.

In many cases a situation analysis is undertaken from the perspective of the total company or product line and will involve finding answers to dozens of questions including the history of product distribution, pricing, packaging, consumer analysis, competition and many more several good planning guides are available on situation analysis. Suffice it to say that situation analysis is generally the foundation for any well-developed marketing programme, and the cornerstone for an advertising plan.

1.3 Advertising Campaign

1.3.1 Meaning

According to the Cambridge Dictionary, an advertising campaign is "a planned series of advertisements that will be used in particular places at particular times in order to advertise a product or service and persuade people to buy it or use it".

An advertising campaign is a series of advertisement messages that share a single idea and theme which make up an integrated marketing communication (IMC), for a particular product, idea, person, event or brand. Advertising campaigns may appear in one or in different media channels across a specific timeframe that is clearly defined. Modern advertising often combine multiple online and offline campaigns.

Advertising campaigns are the groups of advertising messages which are similar in nature. They share same messages and themes placed in different types of medias at some fixed times. The timeframes of advertising campaigns are fixed and specifically defined.

Thus an advertising campaign is an organised course of action to promote a particular product, person, service or event. It employs intentional and carefully coordinated series of marketing tools in order to reach the target audience. This mainly includes a series of advertisements released through different media, sometimes accompanied by additional events and activities. The end purpose of any advertising campaign is to boost awareness of the subject matter and generate demand. The exact structure of the advertising campaign will depend on the nature of the product or cause and the target audience that the campaign is designed to reach.

BusinessDictionary.com has defined an advertising campaign as, "A coordinated series of linked advertisements with a single idea or theme."

An advertising campaign has also been defined as "specific activities designed to promote a product, service or business. It is a coordinated series of steps that can include promotion of a product through different mediums (television, radio, print, online) using a variety of different types of advertisements. The campaign doesn't have to rely solely on advertising, and can also include demonstrations, word of mouth and other interactive techniques".

1.3.2 Basis of Campaign/ Types of Advertising Campaigns

There are basically four types of advertising campaigns.

They are:

1. A Word Hook Advertising Campaign
2. A Character Hook Advertising Campaign
3. A Repeatable Theme Advertising Campaign
4. A Consistent Brand Layout Advertising Campaign

1. **The word hook:** The "word hook" is a catch phrase that is repeated from advertisement to advertisement. One of the greatest examples of a successful word hook advertisement campaign that we witnessed in the recent past was the Word Hook Advertising Campaign around the catch phrase, "Ab Ki Baar Modi Sarkar".

2. **The character hook:** A character hook advertising campaign uses a hero, villain, victim or other characters to embody a key attribute of a brand. A successful advertising campaign using a character hook could be the campaign carried out by McDonald using the character Ronald McDonald, a hero of happiness created in 1963. Ronald helped McDonald's to own the family fast food. The pretty girl of Rasna, made Rasna the drink for every child.

   Characters are very effective for breaking through advertising clutter and establishing emotional connections with the audience. They are vivid, intriguing, and cause people to care about them. If a consumer cares about a character, then he/she will care about the brand.

3. **A repeatable theme:** A repeatable theme is a situation that plays out again and again calling out for the need for a particular product. A classic example is the advertisement of "Idea Cellular network". The advertisement depicts people's predicament in various situations in which each of them has no idea as to how to solve the problem. The solution is given in the punch line "Get Idea".

   Consumers know the punch line that is coming. They love to see the set-up played out in different situations. It is satisfying to be in on the joke, before it comes.

   Repeatable themes make the target customer feel like they have the inside track. They know how to play along and thus feel connected to your brand.

4. **Consistent layout:** A consistent layout uses a unique design look and repeats these elements at each consumer touch point. This allows the consumers to identify the company at a glance. For example the, retail "Central" outlets all over India have the same layout, colour combination, mascot etc. Whether you are at 'Pune Central' or 'Bangalore Central' the layout, design and colour is the same. In a consistent layout what is important is to see that all elements of the layout are as distinct and different from the competitor's layout. This will help your company to stand out in the clutter.

One of the keys to the consistent layout is to be different. If everyone else is using corporate blue, you need to use another colour. If everyone else is doing serious design, you should come up with a mischievous or playful design. Consistent design is about consciously standing out from the crowd and keeping your trademark design going on everything.

When a company uses one design look and feel, customers feel comfortable with that brand faster and for longer. In an uncertain world, the consumer's deep desire for something they can consistently count on is fulfilled by a consistent layout.

1.3.3 Length of Campaign

What is an effective length of time over which to run an advertising campaign? This question does not have a simple answer. The opinions of many advertisers differ on this. However most of the answers fall in the range of six months to one year.

However to better understand the length of time that an advertising campaign should run to be effective we first need to understand the strategy behind an advertising campaign and its execution.

Advertising / Marketing campaigns are broken into two parts:

1. **Strategy:** Strategy is the planning phase where a marketer determines the target audience, the message, what marketing tactics will be used, and how results will be measured.

2. **Execution:** Execution is the action part where the marketer follows through on his plan.

The length of time that an advertising campaign will run will depend upon the strategy used by the marketer, or the type of plan that is earmarked for the execution of the strategy.

Another determinant of the length of campaign could be what the competition is doing. You can have a campaign not just different from the competitor but also longer or shorter depending upon the message you want to send.

Another determinant could be, understanding the consumers and their needs. The marketer can look at the past spending habits and past marketing efforts to determine the length of the campaign. Learning from mistakes is one big part of marketing.

Availability of finance is another important criterion in determining the length of an advertising campaign. If you are a smaller company with limited resources, chances are you do not have money to keep a promotion going for a long time. Larger corporations can afford to extend their marketing campaign if they have budgeted for it.

1.3.4 Parameters Governing Advertising Campaign

Given below are the parameters that govern an advertising campaign:

1. **The total advertising budget:** This is one of the main factors on which depend many aspects of an advertising campaign. The more the finances available the lesser the constraints faced by the advertiser.

2. **Availability of media:** In a general sense, all media are available to the advertiser. The availability of media becomes an issue if the advertiser wants a specific time/space slot.

3. **Consumer profile:** The type and kind of advertising campaign undertaken will depend upon the profile of the consumer.

4. **Product profile:** The kind of product that is to be advertised will determine the advertising campaign. For example, consumer goods and other products that are easy to use will use short advertisements to get the point across. However, technical products that require major explanations will deploy an advertising campaign that will have a major focus on salespersons' calls, exhibitions and demonstrations.

5. **The campaign duration and its timing:** This is another aspect of the advertising campaign that will have to be decided well in advance.

6. **The advertising and marketing objectives:** The advertising campaign should be such that the objectives of the campaign are achieved.

7. **The distribution channel:** The channel partners are important to the marketing organization. They help the organisation in the distribution of the products across the country and the globe. The advertising campaign should be such as to instil pride in the channel members for being associated with the organisation and the brand.

8. **The marketing environment including pressure groups and competitors:** All these have to be taken into account while planning the advertising campaign. The campaign should be as different from the competitors as possible. The advertising campaign must place the product in a better light as compared to the competitor. Care should be taken to see that no marketing communication hurts the sentiments of any groups in the society.

9. **A review of previous advertising promotional effort:** This is actually a very important parameter to be taken into account. Care should be taken to see that all aspects from all previous marketing efforts are taken into account. Marketing is one long learning process. The cost of marketing is huge. The cost of mistakes is much more. And in marketing there is no place for repeat mistakes.

10. **The creative consideration:** The creative aspect has to be taken into account while preparing an advertising campaign. However creativity should be such that it is understood by the common man. Advertising is a mass media and the purpose is to spread the message to all.

1.3.5 Planning of Advertising Campaign

In order to plan a successful advertising campaign, the following steps need to be followed:

1. **The advertising campaign objective:** While planning an advertising campaign the first step is to decide the objective of the advertising campaign. The marketer has to be very clear about the objective that he wishes to achieve through this advertising campaign.

2. **Target audience:** The first step is to decide the target audience. The marketer has to determine the target audience to whom his message is to reach.

3. **The media:** The next decision is to decide which media will be used to deliver the advertiser's message. The media decided will depend upon the finances available and the type of message to be delivered.

4. **The message and design of the advertisement:** Once the target audience is decided, the media to be used to propagate the message is finalised; the marketer must then chalk out the message that will be sent to this target audience, through the particular media. This message should be such that it impacts the target audience. For this to happen, the marketer should have a good knowledge of the particular market segment that he is targeting as well as the knowledge of the behaviour of this particular segment. The design and layout of the message is equally important as it should appeal to the target market. Further the message should be such that the marketer should be able to mould it to fit the various media that he intends to use. Many times there is a conflict, should the message be decided first or the media to be used decided. It is immaterial which comes first and which next. The media is the medium through which the message will reach the audience. The media and the message should be compatible.

5. **Performance measurement:** In the planning stage itself the advertiser must decide how the performance of the advertising campaign will be measured as well as which tools will be used to measure the performance.

1.4 Advertising Agency

1.4.1 Meaning and Definition

An advertising agency has been defined by the American Advertising Agencies Association as:

1. An independent business organisation,
2. Composed of creative and business people,
3. Who develop, prepare and place advertisements on advertising media,
4. For sellers seeking to find customers for their goods and services.

Thus, an advertising agency is an organisation that offers specialised knowledge, skills and experience that is required to produce an effective advertising campaign. It has writers, artists, media experts, researchers, television producers, accounts executives, etc. These specialists work together to understand fully the advertiser's requirements of an advertising campaign and develop suitable plans and strategies. An advertising agency is the fountain-head from which flow most of the advertisements that we see and hear day in and day out. An advertising agency is the centre of the advertising industry.

The term advertising agency is usually shortened as ad agency. They are called as an agency because they are literally the agents of the media who pay them a commission. Thus the media is the principal and the ad agency is the agent of the media. The media pays a higher rate of commission to accredited agencies and a lesser rate to non-accredited agencies.

1.4.2 Services and Functions of an Advertising Agency

An advertising agency basically has two masters. One is the advertiser to whom the agency acts as a consultant, and secondly the media, in which the agency places the advertisements for its clients. As such the functions of the advertising agency can be discussed under two heads, namely client functions and media functions.

(I) Functions for the Client

- **It replaces the advertising department:** When the client hires an advertising agency to plan and execute its advertising campaign, its own advertising department remains merely a co-ordinating and supervisory department acting like a clearing house between the unit and the agency. The agency does practically all the work based on the client feedback or requirements.

- **Objective viewpoint:** The agency being an outsider can take an objective view of the advertiser's plans and proposals and thus plan the advertising campaign accordingly.

- **Use of experts in every field:** The agency has a team of expert and well-trained talent in every field that is required for executing an effective advertising campaign. A client may not be in a position to hire such skilled staff on a permanent basis. However, the agency does. Further the development of advertising campaigns is a result of teamwork. In this respect too, an agency provides opportunity as well as flexibility for various combinations of agency personnel from different departments to form teams to work for specific accounts and client.

- **Use of support systems:** An advertising agency has regular contacts with various support systems required for the production of advertising material. A major advantage of the agency is its regular dealing with the media and the expertise it develops in the process. All this can be used to the advantage of the client.

- **Sharing experience and expertise:** In case a client is not experienced, in such a case the expertise of the advertising agency is a great help to the client. Advertising agency skills are also useful while preparing advertising campaigns that have a higher risk factor. For example, while introducing a new product the risk factor is definitely higher. In such a situation the client can majorly benefit from the experience of the advertising agency, which it has gathered from the number of clients it has served in the past, and the number of new products it has helped to launch.

(II) Functions for the Media

- **It assures risk-free business:** It is the advertising agency that is the 'go between' between the client and the media. It is the agency that buys the time and space in the media. It is the agency that pays the media. This saves the media from the trouble of finding out the credit worthiness of a number of clients, that is, companies. As the agency pays the media there is absolutely no credit risk for the media.

- **It eliminates the need of the media to sell space and time:** As agencies buy space and time in bulk from the media owners for their numerous clients, it saves the media the job of selling space and time to hundreds and thousands of individual advertisers. Instead of numerous advertisers the media has to only deal with a few advertising agencies.

- **The advertising agency performs the job of advertising scheduling:** Releasing the advertisement at the right time and the right place is very important from the point of view of the advertiser who is naturally very interested in getting the best for the amount spent. Advertising scheduling is the most tedious of all jobs involved in the advertising industry. It is the advertising agency that shoulders this responsibility as part of the service package.

- **It cuts down the production cost:** The advertising agency provides the media owners with the ready material for release. For example, in case of magazine advertisements or newspaper for that matter, advertising plates are given to the media for final printing. Thus, the typographers, engravers and the like staff of the media are exempt from their work. Thus, the agency performs most of the work and the media is just to print or release it.

Services performed by Ad Agencies

Thus, the advertising agency performs functions for both the client as well as the media. In addition it also provides some services to the clients which are as under. The advertising agency provides help in:

(i)   Selecting target consumers

(ii) Determining prices and discounts

(iii) Designing products

(iv) Designing packages

(v)   Developing channel of distribution strategies

(vi) Conducting market research projects

Agencies that provide services as mentioned above in essence have become marketing consultants or specialists, as most of these services are non-advertising activities. In fact some organisations virtually turn over the planning and direction of their marketing programmes to advertising agencies.

1.4.3 Factors involved in Agency Selection / Advantages of Advertising Agency

An advertising agency is an outside organisation that gets an absolute insight into the client company. Further the strengths and weakness of the company are revealed to the agency. As such a lot of care and precaution has to be taken while selecting an advertising agency. Some of the factors involved in agency selection are as under:

1. **Services offered:** The first consideration for a potential advertiser is the range of services offered by the advertising agencies. A typical advertising agency starts with the advertising brief given by the client, which is taken through the stages of development of detailed plans, creating campaigns, giving the final form after processing through various stages involving artwork, photography and so forth, and arranging for placement in the various media according to the agreed schedule. An agency would sub-contract some production jobs such as block-making, printing and in some cases photography. However, the overall responsibility of the final output would rest with the agency.

   Some advertising agencies also offer certain additional services as mentioned above. Thus, depending upon the extent of functions and services offered and the requirement of the client, the advertising agency is selected.

2. **Competition:** No advertiser will give his advertising work in the hands of that agency that handles his competitor's accounts. If allowed, it results in a loss instead of a gain for the advertiser. Thus, this aspect has also to be kept in mind.

3. **Location of advertising agency office:** Another major consideration, at least in a country like India, is the location of the office of the agency. A considerable amount of communication, including personal meetings, is required at various stages of decision-making in the development of advertising plans and materials.

   Therefore, it becomes essential for the advertiser to have a ready access to the agency. Some agencies allow a certain periodicity of visits to clients as a part of their normal service. This arrangement is convenient and also economical in terms of time and expenses for the agency, as long as it is in the same location as that of the client. Agencies may charge the client for additional visits by their executives, if required. In such cases outstation clients are at a disadvantage as the costs of regular and additional visits may be an inhibiting factor in choosing an outstation advertising agency, if they have to work within a small budget.

4. **Size of agency:** Another factor to be considered is the size of the advertising agency. Both large and small agencies have a set of advantages and disadvantages to offer. The advantages claimed by large agencies are perfection, wider range of skills and

numerous facilities and services. The limitations are smaller advertisers are not attended, costly service, and lack of personal touch. On the other hand, small agencies are more ambitious and eager, more receptive and enthusiastic than the larger ones. Their merits are quick response to needs, and attention to personal needs and details. Their limitations are lack of specialisation, lack of breadth of knowledge, and absence of quality. However, smaller agencies are usually chosen for their personalised services, which makes the advertiser feel satisfied with the special care and personalised attention that he gets.

5. **Reputation and record:** While selecting an advertising agency, a client will definitely look into the reputation of the agency and choose that one which has an established reputation and goodwill in the market. The sources from which information about the reputation of an agency can be got is media, clients, past and present, and of course, the competitors. Further its records also reflect the reputation of the agency. These records pertain to the clients of the company past and present. Who are/were the clients? How big are/were they? What are/were their problems? What did the agency do for them? How long are/were they with the agency? The answers to all these questions throw light on the track record of the company. It is essential to choose an agency with a good track record and good reputation.

6. **Management:** The management of the agency is perhaps the most important factor to be considered in agency selection. Management is largely a matter of its personnel. While selecting the agency the advertiser checks out the experience and calibre of the top executives. The work done by them in their past jobs as well as the present position speaks for itself. The personnel turnover of the agency is almost as important as the turnover of accounts. Every advertiser is deeply interested in the identity and character of the persons handling his problem on behalf of the agency.

7. **The method of payment:** The charges that the advertising agency is going to charge the advertiser for the services that it renders is also important. There are differences in the ways in which advertising agencies handle the problem of charging their clients for research and certain other services. Thus it is necessary to ascertain exactly what services will be rendered and at what cost. This is important as the advertiser wants to get the best out of the money that he spends.

In a nutshell, all the above factors are to be considered. However, the final selection of an agency is normally a joint decision of the people from the advertising, sales and top management with recommendations of the advertising manager and views of the top management.

1.4.4 Organisational Structure

There is no set organisation structure for all advertising agencies. There are variations and adaptations in the organisation structure of the agencies to suit their individuality. The size of the agency, the functions performed by it, and the personnel employed by it determine its organisation structure. However, one of the following two types of structures is found in virtually every agency. Both have proved to be successful.

1. **The group type of organisation structure**

    In this type of a structure you have a group of individuals servicing a client. The group comprises of an account executive, a copywriter and a layout artist. The group contacts the client/clients and does creative work for them. It uses other central units like media research, mechanical production and accounting as and when it needs them. Some groups serve more than one or two clients at a time. The idea is to make a team of trained individuals for specialised work and let them work on some problem for the same client or other clients. Basically this type of an organisation structure is more suited to large advertising agencies. This type of a structure has also been referred to as a matrix type of an organisation structure.

2. **The department type of organisation structure or concentric agency**

    Under this type of a structure there is a separate department for each advertising function. A specialist in that field heads each department, and the persons in each department are responsible to the head of the department rather than to the accounts executive. Each department directly serves a client, unlike the group structure in which a group coordinates with the client. Thus a copywriter in this type of a structure works for four or five accounts and writes the copy for four or five different products. The account executive calls upon the copy department for the copywriting on his accounts, and the art department for the layouts and illustrations etc.

    Some agencies are a mixture of group and departmentalised types, incorporating certain features of each. There are countless variations and the determining factors are the size, character, and location of the client accounts.

1.4.5 Types of Advertising Agency

Agencies grew in size offering more varied and specialised services. Later in order to cater to the needs of the overseas clients and as more multinational corporations came into being, advertising agencies acquired a multinational character. Simultaneously, some other forms of agencies also came into being. These are:

1. **The boutique agency:** Copywriters and art directors, instead of being tied up with a single agency, set up their own shops to sell the creative function at a fee. These shops came to be known as "boutique agencies".

2. **The a la carte agency:** These agencies sell each individual service on an optional basis for an individual fee.

3. **The in-house agency:** This agency is owned by the advertiser. In fact it is nothing but the advertising department of the advertiser. Large companies have in-house agencies that operate and control the entire advertising programme by themselves. For example, Reliance has Mudra, Malhotras' have Bharat Advertising, Lohia Machines have Shristi etc. When corporations have a variety of products and services to sell and have a multi divisional set up the in-house agency is very economical.

1.4.6 Advertiser and Advertising Agency Interface

From a situation analysis point of view, the advertiser needs to know what kinds of facilitating agencies exist and the nature of the services they provide. From a planning point of view much local advertising is done without the services of an advertising agency or a research supplier. On the other hand, a national advertiser may have under contract many different agencies and research suppliers, each serving one or more brands in a product line. Many advertising decisions involve choosing facilitating agency alternatives.

1. What advertising agency should be chosen?
2. What media should be used?
3. What copy test supplier will be best for our particular situation?

1.5 Advertising Effectiveness

1.5.1 Introduction

How much is our advertising worth? Has it achieved what it set out to achieve? These are questions that are very difficult to answer. This is because advertising is one of the few, if not the only item of expenditure in a company's balance sheet that cannot be measured in terms of its specific contribution towards sales or profitability. The multivariable forces influencing sales makes it almost impossible to measure with any high degree of precision the sales effect of advertising. The techniques of advertising measurement have not been fully developed and are as of now, a high controversial matter. Few experts agree on how advertising actually works or how its effectiveness can be precisely measured. This is true for the traditional television, radio, print and outdoor media.

However advertisements released though the internet are more easily measurable. It is very easy to gather data about the performance of internet ads. When a potential customer clicks on your ad, you can see not only exactly where they came from to get to your site, but also how they then interact once on your site. When enough data is collected you can adjust your marketing plan accordingly.

Advertising is aimed at motivating and affecting consumers' behaviour in a way that is beneficial to the company or brand advertised. If the advertisement achieves its objective then it may be said that the advertisement is effective. The advertisement is as effective as the degree to which it is successful in achieving its objectives.

1.5.2 Objectives of Measuring Advertising Effectiveness

Evaluating advertising effectiveness is necessary to bring out result-oriented advertisement communication. The basic objectives of evaluating advertising effectiveness are as follows:

1. **Value for money**: Advertising is expensive. Most organisations spend huge amounts on advertising. If the advertisement or advertising campaign is unsuccessful, it would mean that the amount spent on the advertising campaign has been wasted. Thus one of the major objectives of measuring the effectiveness of the advertising campaign is to confirm whether the advertising budget was used fruitfully or not.

2. **Determine the reach of the company**: Many a media give you figures of reach. For example, television channels give the TRPs of their shows. Magazines give you circulation figures. This helps the organisation understand to a great extent who and where they are reaching.

3. **To know which aspect of our advertising campaign has reached saturation point**: Those media/techniques that are not yielding any great results can be done away with. Thus the organisation can stop wastage of finance and focus on better avenues that will yield good results.

4. **To know about the competition:** Another objective of measuring the effectiveness of the advertising campaign is to understand the competition's strategies and how we can make use of them to better our advertising campaign.

5. **Planning the next campaign**: Measuring the effectiveness of advertising helps the organisation learn from its past mistakes and plan a better campaign in the future.

1.5.3 Areas of Assessment of Effectiveness

In order to assess the effectiveness of advertising with any degree of accuracy, it is essential to divide the whole process into various stages. The effectiveness of advertising is assessed at each stage of the advertising campaign. In fact, for a product that had a previous advertising campaign, the process of assessment begins from first assessing the effectiveness of the old campaign, making the required changes and moving on to the preparation of a fresh advertising plan keeping in mind the old follies. Thus, carrying out research during the following four stages can do the assessment of the effectiveness of advertising:

1. A continuous analysis of past advertising experience is a very useful first step except in case of new advertisers or products. Such an analysis can provide a valuable basis for reviewing and developing advertising strategy.

2. Surveys of buyer behaviour and consumer preferences are helpful in developing advertising objectives and strategy. Such research will also be useful in monitoring changes in the target audience.

3. The third area involves a pre-testing of the advertisements before they are released. Pre-testing is very important as it provides an indication as to the likely acceptance of the advertisement or campaign by the target market. Results of pre-testing will bring forward the limitations of the advertisement or campaign, and thus, changes can be made before the advertisement is released. This will help the advertiser save on time and money. As media costs form one of the largest items of expenditure in an advertising campaign, a qualitative and quantitative evaluation of media should be done at this stage.

4. The last stage of measuring the effectiveness of an advertisement or advertising campaign is post-test research. Post-test research is concerned with finding out information about how well the advertisement has succeeded in achieving its objective. Post-test research involves testing of the reach and impact of the advertisement after it has been released. Pre-production research and post-production testing are complementary.

It must be clearly understood that advertisement testing is not designed to help in setting a creative strategy or in the development of advertising ideas. Its task is to provide guidance on the relative importance, in terms of consumer interest, of various possible advertising appeals.

1.5.4 Difficulties of Measuring Advertising Effectiveness

1. **Cost:** The most common difficulty in measuring the effectiveness of advertising is the cost of conducting a measurement program. Often companies believe that the money used for measuring their advertising effectiveness can be better spent on creating more advertisements or improving their product.

2. **Research problems:** The evaluation process is sometimes very complicated, time intensive and confusing for a company that is trying to start such an effort. Further it is nearly impossible to evaluate the result of any one aspect of marketing/advertising. Thus it becomes difficult for the marketing managers to justify the amount spent. For example, it might be very difficult to isolate the contribution of the company's banner ad program from their overall marketing effort as a consumer might not necessarily make a purchase based on what they see in banner ads, but consider a variety of factors (brand image, previous experience with the company, or on TV) when making a purchase decision. However, although it might be true that we cannot pinpoint the cost contribution of one program, research can be used to evaluate the communication, reach and other factors associated with each advertising method.

3. **Disagreements on what, when and where to test:** There are a variety of methods used when determining what, where and when to measure the effectiveness of an advertising program. Choosing the appropriate measurement method depends largely on the industry the firm is in, the objectives of the program and the person analysing the results. For example, sales managers may want to measure the contribution of the advertising program on sales, whereas top executives may be interested in the effects of the program on the company's image. These differences often lead to a great deal of confusion between the managers and might lead them to abandon the evaluation program altogether. However, there is no rational reason for this conflict.

1.5.5 Evaluation of Advertising Effectiveness

1. **Pre-placement Evaluation of Advertising**

In order to create a winning advertising campaign, it is essential to test the effectiveness of the advertising campaign right from the time the idea is conceived. Pre-placement evaluation includes the use of a systematic and methodological approach in estimating the possible effectiveness of the advertisement before it is released. Pre-testing helps in avoiding possible negative effects at later stages.

Testing the creative approaches and themes prior to their development, can give an indication as to their effectiveness. Themes, product ideas, brand names, slogans and other elements to be included in the advertisements can thus be evaluated at this stage itself. Pre-testing helps the advertiser to select the best form of advertisement before incurring the expense and risk of presenting it on a full scale run. Pre-tests are intended to discover both the strengths and the weaknesses of an advertising campaign and of the individual advertisements. Pre-placement evaluation of advertising or pre-testing involves testing of the following:

(A) Concept Testing

A major feature of the creative strategy, which affects the ultimate effectiveness of the advertising campaign, is the basic communication concept around which the advertising campaign is to be developed. This concept has to be tested before it is finally chosen. Concept testing would usually involve not more than 50-100 respondents. In concept testing, usually the following techniques would be used. They are:

- **Qualitative Interviews:** Qualitative interviews of an informal nature may be conducted individually or in groups, from amongst people drawn from a cross-section of ages, occupations, and income levels which may represent the audience for the advertisement in question.

- **Free Association Tests:** These tests are used to pick up secondary associations to names or keywords. These tests are conducted by having the respondents mention the first thing that comes to their mind when a given name is mentioned.

- **Statement Comparison Tests:** These are used when the concept is to be tested on small groups. These tests can take on various forms as under:
  - **(i)** **The rank order method:** In this method, the respondents rank the different concepts or themes, thus indicating their preference or desirability in relation to the product.
  - **(ii)** **Paired comparison method:** In this method, the preference of respondents for either of two concepts is determined by using a series of pairs of statements associated with the product characteristics and properties.
  - **(iii)** **The absolute comparison method:** This involves comparison of each of the concepts against an absolute standard. For example, a certain number of features of the product are selected. The advertisement has the option of highlighting a few of these features. Exactly, which feature to highlight, is decided by using this method. This is done be obtaining ratings from a sample of the audience. The audience is asked to rate the various features on a scale of one to ten. These ratings are used to select the features to be highlighted and the features to be dropped.

(B) Theme Testing

No specific guidelines are available for classifying themes for the purpose of analysis and research. Mohan, Mahendra in "A survey of advertising themes," has attempted a classification of advertising themes under the following categories:

1. **Utilitarian theme:** This theme emphasis on the value of the product or service. It aims at providing satisfaction to the customer by providing him value for the money and effort expended on obtaining the product/service.
2. **Focused theme:** This is an extension of the utilitarian scheme. It will appeal to a particular segment of the market.
3. **Informative theme:** This kind of a theme only gives information about the product or service advertised. No other selling message in stressed.
4. **Non-specific theme:** Such a theme contains only a vague message which has only a passing reference to the product or the advertiser.
5. **Achievement orientation theme:** This theme highlights the achievement in terms of sales and profits, or awards won by the advertiser.
6. **Descriptive and projective theme:** This kind is a combination of informative and achievement-orientation themes.
7. **New product, service, scheme or idea:** This kind basically deals in a new product, service, scheme or idea.

(C) The Media Testing

However great the concept and theme around which the advertisement campaign is prepared, it will not be successful if the appropriate media vehicle is not used. Thus, testing the effectiveness of the choice of media is a major part of pre-placement testing. Advertising media used not only has a major effect on the cost of advertising but can also influence advertising effectiveness in the following ways, and hence, is vital to undertake media research in pre-concept testing.

1. The choice of media determines the size and characteristics of the audience exposed to advertising. That is, how many and what type of persons would have an opportunity to see or hear or read the advertisement and how often.

2. The choice of media determines the environment in which the advertisement is viewed, heard or read by the audience. It determines whether the advertisement reaches him when he is in a favourable, unfavourable or neutral mood.

3. Lastly, it is the choice of media that is responsible for the overall impact of the advertisement campaign, namely 'Has the information been communicated as desired?' 'Have the attitudes formed or changed?', 'Has the desired action been taken?' All these are majorly affected by choice of media.

(D) Copy Testing

Another area in which pre-testing is done is the area of copy. Copy testing is carried out in order to establish whether the message content and presentation are likely to perform their desired task or not. Copy testing lets the advertiser know what changes or improvements should be made. Usually, pre-tests for copy are conducted in the following situations:

- To substitute an ongoing campaign with a new campaign
- To introduce a new product or brand
- When there are uncertainties or contradictory views expressed about the content of an advertisement.

A pre-test is usually carried out on a relatively small sample. However, it is very important to simulate the actual environment in which the audience will be exposed to the advertisement. This is especially relevant for pre-tests conducted for television advertisements. Some of the common methods of pre-tests carried out in this area are mentioned below:

(i) **Consumer Jury:** In this technique, a group of people who represent a cross-section of the potential consumer categories are shown the commercial and asked to give their views on specific elements of the content and on the creative approach used. Another way of carrying out this technique is by approaching each individual member of this group separately at their respective residences. The opinions and views of each member are collected and a collective view is later collated to get a representative opinion.

(ii) **Matched Samples:** Two or more groups of persons comparable in respect of parameters such as age, sex, income, occupation, behavioural characteristics, and product usage as relevant to the research problem, constitute matched samples. Under this technique, a change is made in any one element of the advertisement like, the theme, slogan, headline, visual etc., or, one element is changed and the rest is all the same. One advertisement is shown to one group and the other to the other group. Thus, the effect of the changed element is understood.

(iii) Portfolio Tests: This technique is also known as the recall or impact test. Under this technique, a portfolio containing test advertisements or one test advertisement among several control advertisements is placed in the hands of the respondents who are asked to read the advertisements, taking as much or as little time as they want. These respondents are interviewed after they have finished reading the advertisements. After this, the performance of one advertisement as compared to another is evaluated based on the recall of the respondents. The respondent is asked one question after another and the answers determine which advertisements are remembered and which features stand out.

(iv) Storyboard Tests: Storyboard test is a test that is similar to portfolio test. However, a portfolio test is used for testing the effectiveness of advertisements using print media whereas storyboard tests are used for measuring the effectiveness of film/television advertisements. Under this technique, the storyboards are developed into film strips or video cassettes. Respondents are usually shown 8 to 10 such experimental advertisements. After the screening of the advertisements, measurements of recall of products and brands and also of retention and comprehension of messages are made. The respondents may also be asked to make observations on the qualitative features.

(v) Use of Mechanical Devices: Sometimes, mechanical devices are also used to test copy. Some of the devices used are as under:

- **Eye-movement cameras:** These are devices that record the amount of time subjects spend looking at advertisements and the path of the eye as it travels from one element of an advertisement to another.

- **Pupilometric devices:** These record the changing dilation of a subject's pupil while viewing a print advertisement or an advertising film. These changes give an indication of the attention value of an advertisement and the related emotional responses.

However, all the pre-testing techniques described above have certain limitations. There is no established theory of how advertising works. Pre-testing can only offer a limited but valuable indication of what a test advertisement can achieve. Differences in the pre-test setting and the actual situations of exposure to the advertisement can make a substantial impact on the overall effectiveness of the advertisement. This should be taken into account while selecting and designing tests and interpreting results.

2. Post-placement Evaluation of Advertising

Post-tests measure the impact of the message. They seek to discover which advertisements and what elements of various advertisements get the best response, what position produces better results, what medium or issue of a medium pulls better, or how well a whole advertising campaign is progressing. They provide information on whether a brand name or the selling theme of a given advertisement or advertising campaign has penetrated the reader's mind, and the extent of the penetration. Post testing measure the following:

(A) Measure of Audience Exposure

In order to be effective an advertisement must gain exposure. Exposure is the number of target consumers who see or hear the advertiser's message. Without exposure the advertising is doomed for failure. Marketers may obtain an idea of the exposure generated by a medium by examining its circulation or audience data, which reveal the number of print copies sold, the number of persons passing the billboard or riding in transit facilities, the number of persons tuned into at various radio or television channels at various points of time.

Another means of finding out the exposure of advertising is through readership or listener surveys. Here interviewers ask consumers if they have read, viewed or listened to advertisements, while going through a magazine or viewing the television. Readership tests provide a useful supplement to the circulation data, as circulation data do not indicate how many target consumers actually read the advertisement, whereas readership data gives you information about how many readers or viewers of a particular media have actually seen and mentally registered the advertisements.

There are companies that provide information on the exposure of the readers of magazines or newspapers to the advertisements contained in them (readership surveys). Interviewers visit the respondents at houses and ask if they have read a certain magazine. Readers of the concerned magazine are then asked to review page by page the advertisements they remember having seen.

When respondents answer they have seen a particular advertisement, that advertisement is rated as "noted". When respondents answer that they have not only seen a particular advertisement but have realized that the advertisement is for a particular product, such advertisements are rated as "seen-associated". And lastly when the respondents answer that not only have they seen the advertisement but also that they remember most of the advertisement such an advertisement is rated as "read-most". These ratings were first undertaken by Daniel Starch, a pioneer in advertising research, and the ratings have come to be known as "Starch Ratings". Obviously, advertisement that is rated as "read-most" is the most effective and one that is rated as "noted" is the least effective. Such readership, listener surveys are carried out for various media.

(B) Measuring Attitudes and Attitude Change

Advertising is aimed at creating a favourable impression for a company and its products. One of the techniques used to measure the effectiveness of an advertisement after its release in the media is by measuring the changes in the attitudes of the audience, towards the product or the company. Has the desired attitude change taken place or not? Various types of attitude measures are used to answer this question. The target group is asked questions ranging from this willingness to buy the product, or the likelihood of buying, or the extent to which the audience now associates certain features (like ultra modern) with the product. An assessment of attitude change calls for a measurement of attitudes towards the product or organisation in question both before and after the appearance of the advertisement.

Another method used to analyse changes in attitudes are an analysis of recall and enquiries. The assumption here is that one remembers or enquires about matters towards which they hold favourable attitude. Some researchers also use the pupil dilation test in order to evaluate changes in attitudes.

(C) Effect on Sales

Advertising by itself has no direct impact on the sales. This is because advertising together with many other factors affects the sales of the advertised product. Sales are affected by factors such as expansion of the sales force, improved distribution, lessened efforts on the part of the competitors, general improvements in the business conditions and so on. Usually mere increase in sales is not a measure of the effectiveness of advertising. Advertising may be a major factor, a contributing factor or have had little effect on the sales of the product. However there are some cases in which the sales affect of advertising can be used in order to measure the effectiveness of advertising.

1. Direct response by mail or telephone orders: The measurement of the effectiveness of advertising through an increase in sales is possible when the advertisement is so designed as to complete the entire sales transaction. This is what happens in mail order selling. Each advertisement is expected to bring in specific orders for products advertised. The number of such orders received becomes a ready means for evaluating what the advertisement has achieved.

2. Controlled field experiments: A means for measuring the effectiveness of advertising involves the setting up of a controlled experiment within a limited area. An advertising programme is undertaken in one or more test cities. A tabulation of the sales volume is made for the advertised product in the retail stores of these cities before, during and after the test ads are run. At the same time a check is also kept on the sales in one of the controlled cities where no advertisement campaign is conducted. Thus the sales records of the cities where no advertisements are released indicate the sales that would take place in the normal course without advertising. The sales of the test cities show the sales with advertising. Thus the difference in sales in the two cities, that is, the test city and the controlled city can be attributed to advertising. Even when the increase in sales due to advertising is negligent, the advertising may have had the effect of heading off a downward trend in sales. Thus the effectiveness of advertising can be measured through an increase in sales. This technique of experimental control can be used both as a pre-test technique as well as a post-test technique.

Another type of a field experiment carried out in order to measure the effectiveness of advertising is known as "split-run". A "split-run" is a technique used for print advertising. In this technique different versions of an advertisement are prepared and inserted in the same issue of a magazine or a newspaper. However, the different versions are carried by different sets of copies. By means of coupons returned or some other such means, it is determined which advertisement copy pulls best. Thus the effectiveness of a particular advertisement copy can be determined.

Thus the above are the various techniques that can be used to measure the effectiveness of the advertisements after they are released. It is also known as post-testing.

1.6 Advertising Control

1.6.1 Introduction

Ethics is a choice between good and bad, between right and wrong with reference to a particular culture at a given point of time. It represents a set of moral principles and values. 'Moral' principles are the rules or the standards of what is 'right' or 'wrong'. Therefore, morality deals with right or wrong conduct. Morality represents a set of principles of right and wrong behaviour. Here, morality is a more comprehensive term than ethics. This is because moral values include ethical values, but the opposite is not true.

Laws in most countries are stringent against untruth in advertisements. The consumer's conscience also pressurises the advertiser to be ethical. But the most important tool to ensure that an ethical code is followed in advertising is self-control. Let us view how advertisers can themselves exercise self-control in order to make sure that advertising is ethical.

1.6.2 Control of Advertising by Practitioners: Self-Control

Self-control means control exercised by the advertising units or their associations, such as advertisers, advertising agencies and the media owners. These associations of advertisers and media owners play a vital role in curbing anti-social activities. One of the core associations doing this is 'The Advertising Standards Council of India'.

The Advertising Standards Council of India was set up to crack down on misleading and unethical advertisements. It is a non-profit organisation set up by 43 members who are involved with advertising in one way or another. Today, it consists of 78 corporate members, 27 advertisers, 11 press media units, 26 agencies and 7 from allied business. The ASCI puts forward a regulating code. It proposes to adjudicate on whether an advertisement is offensive and its decision will be binding on its members. It proposes to deal with the government if there any disputes.

The Code of the Advertising Standards Authority of India is based on the same lines as the Advertising Standard Council, UK. It seeks to achieve the acceptance of fair advertising practices in the best interests of the consumer.

Guidelines

1. To ensure the truthfulness and honesty of representation and claims made by advertisements and to safeguard against misleading advertisements.
2. To ensure that advertisements are not offensive to generally accepted standards of public decency.
3. To safeguard against indiscriminate use of advertising for promotion of products which are regarded as hazardous to society or, to individuals to a degree or, of a type that is unacceptable to society at large.
4. To ensure that advertisements observe fairness in competition so that the consumers need to be informed on choices in the marketplace and the canons of generally accepted competitive behaviour in business are both served.

Procedures

A 14-member sub-committee of ASCI of people from various walks of life – medicine, law, media – hears a complaint from a member of the public, examines it in the light of the code, asks the advertiser or agency to comment and submit a substantiation. On upholding the complaint by the ASCI, it asks the advertisers to withdraw the advertisement. This entire procedure takes two months.

Shortcomings of ASCI

The ASCI does not have enforcement powers. It acts only as a moral pressure group. Its code is also not definite about offensiveness etc. It lacks resources and its membership though have increased, do not have the desired number as yet.

The ASCI in order to reinforce its powers proposes to publish cases of non-compliance by advertisers and agencies in mass media as well as in the annual report of ASCI. This organisation pre-empts a statutory regulation body and, hence, its survival is in the interest of the profession. ASCI gives the ordinary consumer a chance to complain if misled.

Another organisation of advertisers for self-control is 'The Indian Advertisers Society' whose main aim is to improve the standards and image of advertisements and practice of advertising. We also have the Advertising Agencies Association of India whose main aim is to regulate advertising business. Some other organisations are:

1. Advertising Club, Mumbai.
2. All India Manufacturers Organisation.

The Advertisers Club, Mumbai in collaboration with the International Advertising Association organised a workshop on Code and Self-Regulation in India in April, 1982. The main objectives of the workshop were:

1. To review the self-regulation code on advertising in various countries.
2. To evolve a code of self-regulation in India.

The deliberations of the workshop led to the setting up of a committee on self-regulation code in India and the modalities for its implementations.

In a nutshell, it can be said that the advertising industry should have self-regulation as well as government and consumer regulation as a back-up, so as to ensure that advertisements and advertising industry which is the core of all business today protects the consumer, his interests and, society, in general.

Points to Remember

- Advertising is any paid form of non-personal presentation of ideas, goods or services by an identified sponsor.
- Aspects of advertising
  1. Any form
  2. Paid form
  3. Non-personal
  4. Identified sponsor

- **Functions of advertising**
  1. Information function
  2. Precipitation function
  3. Persuasive function
  4. Reinforcement function
  5. Reminder function
  6. Value-adding function

- **Classification/Types of advertising**

  Advertising can be basically classified into categories:
  1. Product-related advertising
     (a) Pioneering advertising
     (b) Competitive advertising
     (c) Retentive advertising
     (d) Institutional advertising
  2. Public relations institutional advertising
  3. Public service institutional advertising
  4. Patronage institutional advertising

Questions for Discussion

1. Define advertising.
2. State the nature of advertising.
3. State the scope of advertising.
4. What do you mean by advertising objectives?
5. Explain the role of advertising in modern business.
6. Explain the various ethics in advertising.
7. Explain advertising and marketing mix.
8. Explain the various functions of advertising.
9. Explain the benefits and limitations of advertising.

■■■

Chapter **2...**

Copy Decisions

Contents ...

Learning Objectives ...

- To discuss the meaning, objectives, elements, features and types of advertising copy
- To study the principles, components, visualization and format of advertising layout
- To understand the approaches, principles and styles of copy creation
- To learn the pre-testing methods and measurements of advertising copy

2.1 Advertising Copy

2.1.1 Meaning

The word 'copy' has a specific meaning in the world of advertising. An advertising copy is all the written or spoken matter in an advertisement expressed in words or sentences and figures designed to convey the desired message to the target consumers. Strictly speaking the written content of the advertisement is called the copy and the visual parts are called the illustration. However an 'advertisement copy' is the product of the collective efforts of copywriters and artists and the layout men. Copywriters and artists must collaborate to make an advertisement copy. Though copy precedes artwork and layout, in an advertisement copy, the illustration is an element. Therefore an advertisement copy is the written and visual content of an advertisement message or theme.

2.1.2 Objectives of an Advertising Copy

Advertising objectives must be set to guide the creation of advertisements. Without objectives it becomes difficult to measure the results of the advertisements. Advertising objectives are basically of two types namely direct action and indirect action.

When the objective of an advertisement is to cause a direct action, it is known as direct action objective. Direct action means direct action on the part of the consumer. Thus an advertisement is said to have a direct action objective when the consumer responds to it as soon as he sees the advertisement. That is, he decides to do what the advertisement is asking him to do. The majority of retail advertisements and those of direct advertising aim at direct action. Such advertisement copies include coupons for soliciting enquiries. In such copies the unique selling proposition is very strongly presented so as to generate quick and instant response from the prospect; otherwise some special offer or scheme is offered to the prospect, or a free gift or subscription for a limited period of time. All this is done so as to ensure immediate action.

When the advertisement copy is so created that its objective is to establish a favourable attitude of the prospects towards the company, so that this attitude in future leads to buying action, the advertisement copy is said to have an "indirect action objective". This kind of an advertisement copy imprints the name of the company, its products and brands on the mind of the prospects in such a way that whenever in future a purchase action is undertaken, the products of the company are chosen above its competitors. The majority of the institutional and product advertisements aim at indirect action. That is, the prospect knows about the company and its products and will buy it in due course of time.

2.1.3 Features/Essentials of a Good Copy

A good and effective advertisement copy is one that succeeds in reaching the target consumers to create a favourable attitude towards the product and the producer impelling an action. In order to do this a copy should have the following basic requisites or essentials.

1. **It should be brief:** The advertisement copy should be brief yet effective. Most of the readers are interested in shorter advertisements. Advertisements should not be longer than necessary.

2. **It should be dear:** A good advertisement copy should be clear. A clear copy is one that is easily and quickly understood by the readers. The copy should be self-explanatory. The clarity of the copy is affected by using words whose meanings are not understood by the readers, by using incorrect words or the use of ambiguous phraseology. Thus care should be taken to see that such words and phrases are not used.

3. **It should be apt:** An apt copy is one that matches the needs of the prospects. The copy will be more effective if the product features that it portrays match the needs of the prospects. Writing an apt copy is the art of putting words that create a strong desire to possess the product.

4. **It should be personal:** A copy in order to be effective should have the personal touch. This comes by using words like you and yours. Instead of delivering a common message like "Dettol guards health", a personal message like "Guard your health with Dettol" will work better.

5. **It should be honest:** The advertisement copy should avoid dishonest statements and should be truthful. One of the sure ways of winning the hearts of many good customers is to talk of the limitations of the product directly. Thus manufacturers of textiles should admit to colour fading or shrinkage to a certain extent.

6. **It should conform:** Every advertisement copy should conform to standards, rules and regulations acceptable to the advertising media and the laws of the land. Everywhere in the world, no copy is acceptable to any media that offends morality, lacks decency and inflames religious susceptibilities of the people.

Thus the above are the requisites of an effective advertising copy.

2.1.4 Types of Copy

The classification of advertising copies differs from expert to expert in the realm of advertising. However, broadly there can be types of copies as under:

1. **Institutional copy (Fig. 2.1)**

   An institutional copy is one whose main aim is to build up a reputation for the selling house or its departments. It is one that invites the prospects to check the selling outlets at their convenience, and to verify the policies, customer services, conveniences and the superiority of the company over its rivals. It seeks to build goodwill through its philosophies, objectives, and policies towards consumers, employees, government and the community in general so that the prospect remembers the company with a favourable attitude. It is more a public relations advertisement copy.

Fig. 2.1

2. **Reason to copy (Fig. 2.2)**

   Here is a reason why copy provides various reasons as to why a particular product or service offered by the advertiser should be bought. By stressing on the various points of product superiority, it endeavours to convince and persuade the reader in preference of the rival product. This kind of a copy appeals straight to the intellect or judgement of the individual. It tries to prove the superiority of its product by means of evidence in the form of performance tests, records guarantees, survey findings etc.

Fig. 2.2

3. **Human interest copy**

   A human interest copy appeals to the emotions and the senses rather than the intellect and judgement. Sympathy, affection, love, fear, humour, curiosity and other emotional appeals are used in this copy. Human-interest copy talks about the product in relation to people rather than talk hard facts. It comes to the selling points in a roundabout fashion. This type of a copy capitalises on people's unfailing interest in themselves. The human interest copy can take various forms and some of them are as under:

(a) Humorous copy: A humorous copy fully exploits the sense of humour. This copy elicits fun, mirth and laughter. Humour can be successfully used for creating a good copy. However it should be used carefully as various people have different sense of humour. To some gross humour might appeal. Others like a subtle dose of humour. Thus care should be exercised when humour is used to see that the right dosage of humour as required by the target audience is injected into the copy.

Fig. 2.3

(b) Fear copy: Fear is something we all feel at one time or another in our lives. Once aroused, it can haunt our lives, real and imaginary. Fear basically results in a feeling of insecurity about selves, our loved ones and our belongings. A fear copy appeals to the sense of fear and arouses a keen interest in protecting our life and property from the source of fear. It should be carefully used so that the prospect does not associate unpleasantness with the advertiser. In fact it should be used in such a way that the advertiser appears to be the magician who takes away unpleasantness.

(c) Story copy: Narrating a story to inculcate certain values is a technique that is as old as mankind. In the story copy tool, the advertiser uses a story to get people attracted towards his product. The product or service offered by the advertiser forms the central theme of the story. An advertisement copy to be a story copy must be capable of creating a dramatic and vivid impact about the product, service or the advertiser.

(d) Predicament copy: A predicament copy usually overlaps the other three kinds of human interest copies. Such a copy highlights a consumer predicament, discovers solutions, resolves the predicament and then suggests the product use.

4. **Educational copy (Fig. 2.4)**

   A copy that is designed to educate the prospect is known as an educational copy. This kind of a copy is used to inform the prospects about a new product that has been introduced in the market or it may inform the prospects about the changes made in an existing product. This type of copy may be an introductory one or a missionary one. When it informs prospects about the introduction of a new product it is known as an introductory educational copy. When it informs people about changes made in an existing product it is a missionary copy. An introductory educational copy may also be a teaser. Such an advertisement copy does not contain any message except the symbol of the advertiser. The intention is to arouse the curiosity of the reader and thus to stimulate an interest in the forthcoming product. Such advertisements are run in the media at close intervals and contain little or no identification. Then when the curiosity of the public is at its height the name of the product is finally revealed. On the other hand a missionary advertisement copy depicts the possible improvements in the existing product in terms of structure, colour, size and utility. Since the product is known it is sufficient to remind the prospects of its existence and improvements.

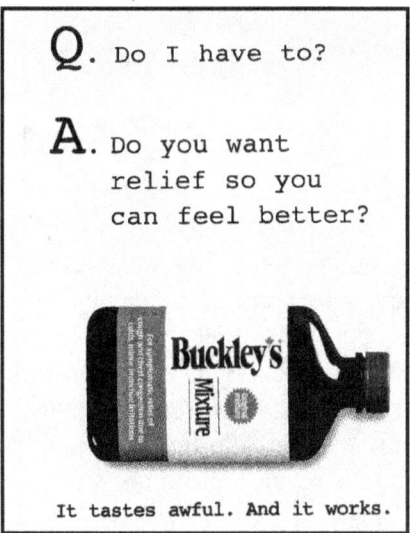

Fig. 2.4

5. **Suggestive copy**

   A suggestive copy tries to suggest or pinpoint or convey the message of the advertiser to the readers. Such a copy may be a direct suggestive copy or an indirect suggestive copy.

(a) Direct suggestive copy: A direct suggestive copy makes statements about the product or service straight to the target audience. It appeals to the prospects directly. However it does not tell him or her to buy the product. (Fig. 2.5)

Fig. 2.5

(b) Indirect suggestive copy: Such a copy does not address the reader directly. It talks on behalf of the reader and the reader is supposed to grasp it in his own interest. In other words it suggests to him indirectly to buy the product or service advertised. (Fig. 2.6)

Fig. 2.6

6. Expository copy (Fig. 2.7)

An expository copy is totally opposite of the suggestive copy. It reveals what the suggestive copy conceals. It is so open that facts are given in very simple and clear way so that there is no need for interpretation. The information given is so clear and concise that it does not tax the brain of the reader at all. Even for a man or woman of below average understanding a cursory glance is enough to perceive, pick and act.

Fig. 2.7

7. Scientific copy

In this copy, the technical specifications of a product are explained. The merits of the product are described in scientific terms. It gives a conviction value to the copy. Basically drugs and medicines are sold through scientific copy. The data inspires confidence both among the lay people and the professionals.

8. Topical copy

When the copy is integrated to a recent happening or event, it is said to be a topical copy. Mostly political events, national sports, world events, parliament news all get extended to the advertisement copy. These days many advertisements portray Miss Worlds and Miss Universe and 'Crorepati' of Kaun Banega Crorepati.

9. Endorsement copy/Testimonial copy (Fig. 2.8)

In these copies, a product is endorsed by an opinion leader who has a large following. The choice of opinion leader depends on the product. Mostly celebrities like famous sports persons and film stars are used to promote the products. Thus you have Juhi Chawla promoting 'Lux' and Rahul Dravid promoting 'Castrol GTX', Hrithik Roshan promoting 'John Players' and Shah Rukh Khan promoting 'Pepsi'. Sachin has promoted a number of products and so have Gavaskar and Kapil Dev. The list is endless. Professionals such as doctors, nurses, dentists are also used to endorse products.

Fig. 2.8

2.2 Advertising Layout

2.2.1 Meaning

The final advertisement is a combination of a number of units such as the headline, sub-headline, border, caption, illustration, text and so on. All these are known as the elements of layout. Each element of the layout is so arranged so as to bring about the desired effect in the final advertisement. The layout is the format in which the various elements of the advertisement are combined. The layout is thus a visual representation of the ideas of the creator of the advertisement.

According to **Mr. Otto Klepper**, renowned advertising consultant, "layout" means two things; in one sense, it means the total appearance of the advertisement, that is, its design, and the composition of its elements; in another sense, it means the physical rendering of the design for the advertisement, that is, the blueprint for production purposes. Layout is a drawing of some kind that stimulates the finished advertisement and is called a 'rough', 'sketch', 'visual', 'comp', 'dummy', or a 'story-board'.

A layout plan indicates the following:
1. The shape, the size and the location of the illustration.
2. The style and the size of the type to be used.
3. The space, the headline, sub-headlines and the mass the type is to occupy.
4. The border style.
5. The width of the margin and the white space.
6. Colours to be used for the type, illustration, border and space.
7. Additional directions to the typesetter for executing the plan.

2.2.2 Principles of Advertising Layout/ Layout Format

The three principles of an advertising layout are:
1. Balance in layout
2. Weight
3. Movement

Balance is of considerable importance in layout. This is because the effectiveness of a layout depends almost entirely upon the degree to which it is "balanced" or upon the nicety with which it is thrown off balance. How a layout is balanced depends upon the placement of the various elements around the optical center. Each element of layout has a weight. Here let us understand what is meant by optical center and what is meant by weight.

Optical Centre: In advertising, the optical center is that point where the eye would first rest when it first sees a page. This optical center lies on a vertical line one-third above the actual center of the space. (i.e. the entire advertising space) or page. It is the optical centre that receives the maximum attention and hence the important elements of the advertisement layout are usually placed at this point.

Weight: The weight of the different elements depends upon the colour, size, shape, and type. The bigger the size of the element, the greater will be its weight. The darker the colour of the element the greater its weight. The more closer that an element is to the optical center of the advertisement the greater will be its weight. Thus, the weight of an element can be increased by changing it from a light colour to a darker shade. Or it can be increased by moving it closer to the optical center. Similarly the weight of an element can also be increased by giving it more space i.e. by increasing its size. And vice versa for decreasing its weight.

Basically an advertisement can have a formal balance or an informal balance.

A formal balance or a symmetrical balance is achieved when the two halves of the advertisement that is the left and right, top and bottom have nearly the same weight and are symmetrical. Formal balance is basically the placing of the elements symmetrically with the left side the same as the right side. (Your face is a good example of symmetry. The left side is the same as the right side). A formal balance is used when dignity and stability have to be communicated, especially in case of institutional advertising. When a formal balance is used all the elements are equally balanced around the optical center.

Informal balance is placing the elements in balance around the optical center asymmetrically. In an informal balance the artist does not told the optical center as the focal point around which the elements of the advertisement are placed. In this layout different weights may be used around the optical center and this makes it striking to the reader. An informal balance is used when attention has to be grabbed immediately and interest generated. This kind of a layout is generally used to present unusual and of offbeat ideas.

A study of balance in layout does not revolve only upon studying the weight of the elements and the way they are placed. Equal importance is to be given to movement. In fact movement may even bring balance to a layout that may be unevenly weighted.

Here let us understand what is movement. Movement is any arrangement of the elements, which directs the eye of the reader along a pre-determined path, to the advantage of the advertiser. Movement should encourage the path of the eye in a definite and desired sequence. Here it should be understood that movement means complete movement. The eye must be encouraged along an unbroken path. In planning a movement, it is helpful to lay down the point at which the eye begins its journey and the point at which the journey is intended to end. Before the layout is finalised it should be checked to see whether the movement has been completed in such a manner as to enable the eye to register the desired impression upon the reader's mind.

To conclude it may be said that balance may be symmetrical i.e. mathematically balanced, or asymmetrical i.e. determined by our sense of balance. Balance is influenced by the major factors of weight and/or movement.

2.2.3 Functions of Layout

A layout is the final packet of all the components of the advertisement placed in the size and place in which they will be giving the desired result. A layout is exceptionally important as it performs the following functions:

1. **Attracts the attention of the prospects:** It is the layout that ranges or organises the various elements in an advertisement in such a way as to have the desired effect. It indicates the size and place of each element. Such a placement or organisation gives each element a definite get-up. It is the layout that attracts the attention of the prospect and holds their attention as their vision is guided from one element to another in a logical manner that was desired by the layout designer.

2. **It brings together the copywriter and the art director:** Each advertisement is the outcome of various specialised and talented people like visualisers, art directors, photographers, copywriters, printers etc. In the early stages, the layout serves as a basis for discussion between the copywriter and the art director to see whether the objectives of the advertisement are being achieved or not. Of all the specialists, the copywriter and the art director are at the forefront as they are responsible for the verbal and visual presentation of the advertising message or theme.

3. **It enables the advertiser to visualise his future advertisement:** The layout enables the advertiser and the various others involved to foresee how the final advertisement will look. In fact the rough layout circulates in the various creative departments of the agency, and if any changes are required they can be made. The client is also shown the rough layout, which in fact leaves nothing to the imagination, thus the client can have an exact notion of how the final advertisement will look like. Thus, if the client wants any changes to be made they can be made at this stage itself with the minimum amount of difficulty and cost.

4. **The layout guides the specialist:** The layout guides all the specialists such as the typesetters, printers and other craftsmen who actually prepare the advertisement for use in print. The scope for misunderstandings is very much narrowed down as the layout gives a clear idea to all about exactly what is to be done. The idea visualised is realised only when the layout instructions are followed strictly.

2.2.4 Components of Advertising Layout

The layout of an advertisement is made up of the following components. Let us here study each of the components or elements of the layout in brief.

1. Background (Fig. 2.9)

Fig. 2.9

The term 'background' denotes the backdrop against which the advertisement is placed. The theme of the advertisement should match with the background. In fact, the background provides the theme. Just as a diamond requires the right setting to be fully appreciated, an advertisement also requires the right background. The advertisement of a high-class product will not fit in with the background of a slum area. This product will require the background of an executive office or some such other place. Sometimes, a plain background is used and, at other times, the other elements of the layout are superimposed on a pictorial background.

A background in an advertisement is more important when the picture is scenic and suggests a locale, a place with atmosphere, scale and relationship. For example, an airplane without the background of sky and mountain range or sky and sea will not have the desired effect. The background stimulates the reader's imagination and arouses an interest. It is said that females take more of an interest in backgrounds than the males.

2. Border (Fig. 2.10)

What frames do for pictures, so does border for the advertisement. In fact, the border can be defined as the 'frame' of the advertisement. The border may be light or heavy, obvious or unobtrusive, plain or fanciful, useless or useful. Broadly speaking, the modern trend is towards the elimination of the border.

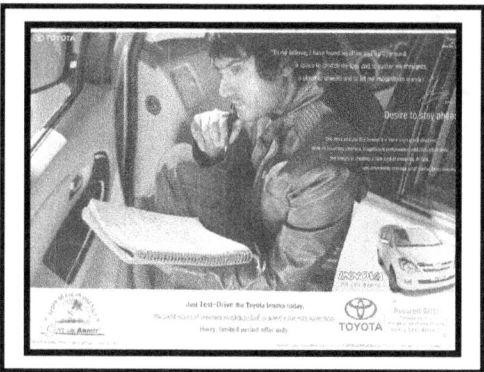

Fig. 2.10

In formal announcements, borders are used in a uniform way so as to make the identification of the advertiser easy. The border may also contain a logo or a name plate or both.

3. Caption (Fig. 2.11)

The word caption is used to describe the subtitle. However, more specifically, the caption is the description of the subhead that appears with an illustration. However, the use of captions is rare in advertising. This is because an illustration in advertising has to be self-explanatory; it has to tell its story quickly, clearly and decisively.

Fig. 2.11

4. Decoration

The earliest use of decoration in advertisements was done when a different type set was used in order to add some ornamentation to the advertisement. Today, however, with the use of computers in the printing technology, a variety of fonts are available for the typesetter to use in order to add decoration to his advertisement. Using different fonts is not the only way of adding decoration to the advertisement. Sometimes, the layout man adds some decorations in the form of pictures to supplement the message of the advertisement. A good example of this is the 'picture book' type of advertisements. In these advertisements, the copy which is brief is set boldly in widely spaced lines; these lines are broken at intervals by placing small pictures. This style of decorating advertisements has been used in the USA. However, it has not found much usage in India.

Fig. 2.12

5.   **Heading (Fig. 2.12 and 2.13)**

Fig. 2.13

A headline is the main door to the entire building of advertisement. It is the title of the advertisement. In fact, title would be a more appropriate term for it, as there is no hard and fast rule that the heading should appear at the 'head' of the advertisement. The headline is the one that stands out in the copy by the size or the style of the type in which it is set, the prominence of its location or the white space surrounding it. It is that word or phrase or sentence that is printed in large sized letters and implies the message that is underlined in the advertisement.

It is the essence, boiled down from the substance of the advertising message.

In dealing with the technique of the heading, there are varied opinions. In contradiction of the rule that the heading should be short, we daily come across long headlines, and in successful advertising campaigns. Thus, what is important is not the size of the heading but what it has to say and the support provided to it by the other elements of layout.

Here, let us dispel the popular illusion that the heading is an essential unit. (Indeed, we are given to understand that when an advertisement appears without one, it is usually because the layout man is 'short of ideas'!) The truth is that convention demands a heading. But brilliant advertising men can come up with campaigns without one.

The headline due to its unique position of prominence in the advertisement performs the following functions.

- It attracts the attention of the reader.
- It induces the reader to read the text.
- It gives the entire message of the advertisement to the reader in a concise manner.

6. Illustration (Fig. 2.14)

Illustration is the pictorial representation of a given text or matter. It may be a drawing, a photograph, a chart, a diagram, or a painting used to gain attention, comprehension and behaviour change. Idiomatically, 'a picture is worth a thousand words'. Pictures are the nearest thing to a universal language. Pictures can do what words cannot. However, in the study of advertising layout, it is easier to regard the dominating picture as the illustration and the other pictures as supports. This helps the layout man to build his layout on the central theme and overemphasis on the subsidiary matter is avoided. The illustration is a very powerful force that shapes the character, personality and tone of the advertisement. The illustration fills the gaps left by the copy. It is the illustration that furthers the advertiser's objective by enhancing the basic selling ideas.

Fig. 2.14

Illustrations are a very important element of layout. Nearly eighty-five percent of the advertisements released today have this element. It is important as it has the power not only to capture the attention of the reader but it also contributes to the theme of the advertisement. The use of illustrations makes the advertisement richer as people are naturally inclined towards pictures. Many advertisements are not read at all, but still the pictures create an impact. Pictures give credibility to the advertisement. They convey the idea quickly and conveniently, and also encourage the reader to read the advertisement in its entirety.

7. Mascot

The mascot is the illustration of a real or imaginary figure or personality introduced into the advertisement to personalise the sales message or the name of the product or service. The mascot is also known as the 'trade character', or 'trade figure'. Examples of mascots are the Maharaja of Air India, Raju of Asian Games, dancing girl of Nirma, etc. From the study of mascots in present day advertising, two principles are seen:

- The mascot must be used constantly if it is to become a useful and telling medium of expression.
- There must be a definite continuity in all layouts embodying the mascot.

8. Product (Fig. 2.15)

A product as an element of layout is the picture of the product that is offered for sale. A product may be featured in startling isolation or, it may be thrown up by a heavy or futuristic background, or by decoration. In other layouts, a number of products may be arranged together so as to give an artistic angle. Another way of showing the product is showing it in use. Showing the product in use or action makes a dramatic impact on the readers. That is why an advertisement of a ready-made shirt, does not show the shirt in isolation, but being worn by a smart male. Showing the product in action has the effect of convincing the prospects about the utility of the product.

Usually, a product is shown in isolation when it is newly introduced into the market and the image of the product and the company has to be established in the minds of the public.

9. Price

Price is considered as a separate unit of layout when it is featured in a type larger and heavier than the body type. With the exception of bargain sale announcements, price is seldom the dominating feature of the layout. Price as an element of layout is usually used only when lower prices are is a dominating argument of the advertisement. However, as far as possible, advertisers refrain from using this argument as in the words of Bolling, "It is impossible to conduct a successful advertising campaign with cheapness as the principal argument in favour of the goods offered ...... for cheapness does not create permanent goodwill."

10. Slogan

Fig. 2.15

A slogan is any word or a group of words used regularly by the advertiser to impress the readers about the basic idea of his product or service. It is the sales argument for a product or service expressed in a few words. It is an original catch phrase that associates selling idea with the product or service. However, sometimes, it can just be a catchy musical jingle, or a sweet sounding note.

The position of the slogan in the layout must be determined on the basis of its relevance to the advertiser's message. When the slogan constitutes the advertiser's message, it is given a place of prominence in the layout. However, when the slogan is just a catchy something, its place is obviously at the bottom of the advertisement layout near the name and logo.

Even though as mentioned above, when the slogan contains the essence of the advertiser's message, and is placed in a prominent position, there is a difference between a headline and slogan. Such a prominently placed slogan may be a headline. Thus, slogans can be good headlines. But headlines are not good slogans. The following are some examples of good slogans:

- *I love you Rasna*
- *Kelvinator, the coolest one*
- *Timekeepers of the Nation ...... Hindustan Machine Tools Ltd.*
- *Hamara Bajaj*
- *The complete man: Raymond*

11. Space (Fig. 2.16)

As an element of layout space means the empty space that is left after all the elements are placed in the layout. Sometimes, just one or two important elements are placed and the rest is just empty space or white space. This is done so as to draw the attention of the prospects only to those important couple of elements. Space is also used to describe the entire space in a publication bought by an advertiser.

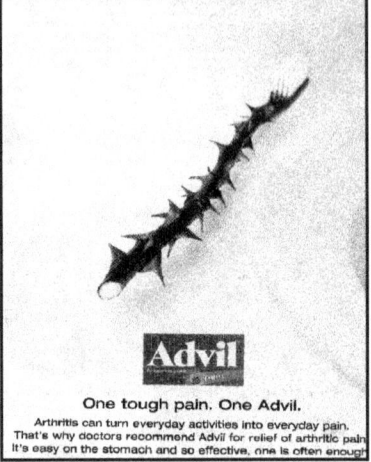

Fig. 2.16

12. Subheading (Fig. 2.17)

A sub-headline is a secondary headline. It expands on the idea of the main headline and carries the interest of the reader a step further into the copy story. It continues, clarifies, and completes the headline. Sometimes, the subhead is also used to 'pick out' the various selling points contained in the text. In such cases, a number of subheads are used and each talks about a particular selling point.

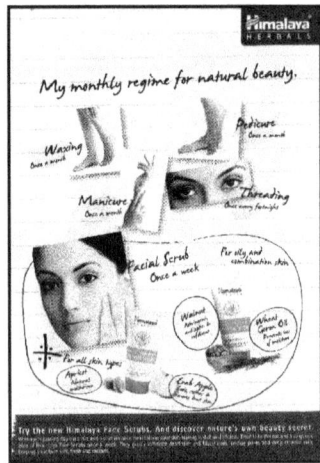

Fig. 2.17

For the use of subheadings, two guiding rules must be kept in mind. They are:

- Use them sparingly.
- Use them to pick out the selling points in the text only when the text is too heavy to invite attention otherwise.

13. Text (Fig. 2.18)

The 'text' or the body of the advertisement is a term that is loosely used to mean the general reading matter or copy. It is the copy that develops the ideas hidden in the headline and expanded by the subheads. If the headline captures the interest of the prospect, it is the text matter that converts that interest into product interest. It is the 'text' or 'body of the copy' that gets a prospect to desire the product by convincing him about the basic worth of the product or service offered.

Usually, it is the headline, subheads and illustrations that are looked at by the readers of newspapers and magazines. However, there are some serious buyers who are really interested to go through the entire sales message.

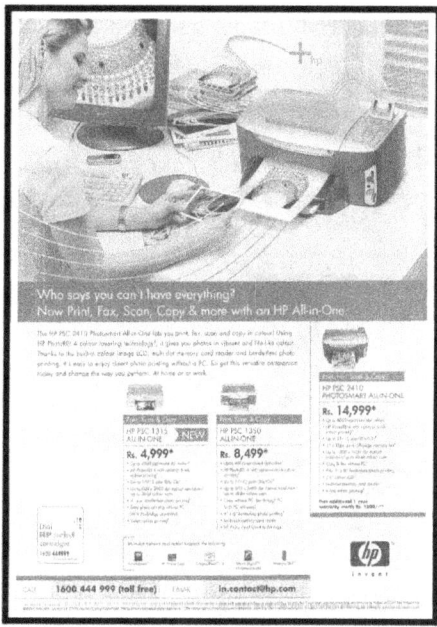

Fig. 2.18

In order to get the desired results out of the body of the copy, the following guidelines should be observed while drafting the text:

(a) Write the text in simple language, carrying the style of a 'personal letter'.

(b) Arrange ideas in order of priority.

(c) Repeat the key ideas in various guises.

(d) Make use of your 'attitude' and replace words like 'we', 'our', and 'ours' with 'you', 'your' and 'yours'.

(e) Present full and specific information.

(f) Never misrepresent the facts.

(g) Determine the suitable length of the copy. The copy should be just long enough to move the prospect to action. Generally, the shorter copy is better. However, in cases where much information is a must, it can be lengthier. Lengthy copy is justified so long as it meets the requirements of the reader.

(h) Call for buying action on the part of the prospect at the closing part of the copy.

In short, a good copy should be clear, simple, compact, arresting and believable. It should draw not only the attention of the prospect but also lead him into action.

14. Identification Marks

Identification mark is the last part of an advertisement copy. It is this identification mark that identifies the particular product or manufacturer and differentiates the product from other similar products. The identification marks help the prospects in identifying the product and the producers precisely and correctly.

Fig. 2.19

Identification marks are lumped under three groups, namely, **'trade name'**, **'brand name'** and **'trademark'**. 'Trade name' or commercial name is the name of the company that makes the product; 'brand name' is the name or a word or words used to identify a particular product. Thus, Cadbury is the trade name of a manufacturer of chocolates. 5 Star is the brand name of a particular chocolate manufactured by Cadbury. Dairy Milk is the brand name of another chocolate variety manufactured by Cadbury. Usually, products are known by their brand names, and an advertisement copy carries the brand name of the product advertised. However, the trade name and address of the company is also sometimes given. This is carried at the end of the advertisement for trade enquiries and solicitation.

'**Trademark**' is a word, symbol or a device used to identify a manufacturer, goods or services and distinguishes them from those of others. The term 'trademark' is broader than the term 'trade name' as the trademark may contain the trade name as a part of it.

Both 'trademark' and 'brand name' can be registered. In fact, they should be registered, as registration gives the following benefits:

1. Constructive notice of ownership claim.

2. Open and conclusive evidence of exclusive right of use.

One more term which is very closely related to the above-mentioned terms is 'logotype'. 'Logotype' is the distinctive symbol representing the name or initials of an organisation, lettered or coloured in a characteristic way and often boxed within a special shape. Logo becomes a part of the house style or livery. It may be registered as a trademark. It is the condensed form of company name or a symbol or the combination of both used to identify the producer of a product or the product range.

Thus, the above are the various elements that are used to make an effective advertisement copy. The layout artist might use just one or two or all the elements depending upon the message to be conveyed. What is important is not the number of elements used but how effectively they are used.

2.2.5 Visualisation of Ad Layout

Basically, an advertisement is an expression of an idea and the success of the advertisement rests on the way in which the idea is expressed in terms of pictures and words used, and the total message. According to **Prof. Maurice I. Mandell**, the term 'visualisation', refers to "seeing in the mind's eye the form of the idea as it would appear in the advertisement". In very simple words, visualisation is the process of designing the advertisement. The ultimate outcome of the process of visualisation is the layout.

A visualiser decides about the inclusion of different elements at the beginning of his work. His questions are: Whether my advertisement will have a headline? Whether there will be a sub-headline? Whether there would be a body copy? Whether to have illustration or a photograph? Whether to include a slogan? etc.

At the second step, he foresees how all these elements will be appearing in the copy. The basic elements with which a visualiser works are headline, sub- headline, body copy, illustration, logo, slogans, border and background, price, product etc.

At the beginning of his work, the visualiser becomes intimate with the copy. In fact, the visualisation process is actually shared by the copywriter and the creative director of visualisation. They decide whether the product should be featured; whether people should be featured; what they would be doing; will there be a background? What type of background should be used? Are photos be used or not? Are sketches be used? How large should the headline be? Where should it be placed? Which components should be included in the final copy? The product? The slogan? The name and address of the company?

Once the visualiser becomes clear about the components or elements, he tries to figure out the correlation that each component or element has with one another. How would they be placed in the copy? How will the final product (advertisement copy) look like?

Essentially, visualisation is a mental process of creating images of a well- balanced whole made up of different elements. On paper, he makes thumbnails which are rough sketches of the various alternatives. This paperwork is the starting point of the process of layout.

One should note the difference between 'visualisation' and 'layout'. Visualisation is the work of copywriters and the creative director. Layout is the arrangement of the various elements or components in the places thought of by the visualisers. Visualisation precedes layout. If visualisation tells 'what', the layout will say 'where'. Layout is the outcome of visualisation. Visualisation is the process of screening the various ways of expressing an idea visually, while layout is about weighing and arranging the various elements of a given advertisement.

2.3 Copy Creation

2.3.1 Introduction

An advertising copy is all the written or spoken matter in an advertisement expressed in words or sentences and figures designed to convey the desired message to the target consumers. Strictly speaking the written content of the advertisement is called the copy and the visual parts are called the illustration. However an 'advertisement copy' is the product of the collective efforts of copywriters and artists and the layout men. Copywriters and artists must collaborate to make an advertisement copy. Though copy precedes art work and layout, in an advertisement copy, the illustration is an element. Therefore an advertisement copy is the written and visual content of an advertisement message or theme.

2.3.2 Principles

1. **Meet the Objective:** The first principle in the creation of the copy is that it should meet the objective of the advertising campaign. The theme of the copy should be consistent with the objective of the advertising campaign.

2. **Sell the Objective:** The copy should be so structured that it not only meets the objective but gets the desired results from the consumers.

2.3.3 Verbal versus Visual Thinkers

Most thoughts happen through the medium of language. We use language as a primary means of communicating thoughts, ideas, and emotions with one another. We are taught early on to read and write.

However we should remember that linguistic thinking or verbal thinking is only one form of thought. As philosopher Martin Heidegger asserts, "What is spoken is never, and in no language, what is said." What is spoken leaves out what is seen. And that which is seen, speaks.

Visual language is an amazingly powerful means of communication. Certainly advertising agencies have realised this. They utilise this knowledge to a great degree. Visual language suffers the same limitations as spoken language. Context is important and with context comes the ability to read between the lines.

A visual language is a set of practices by which images can be used to communicate concepts. Creation of an image to communicate an idea presupposes the use of a visual language. Just as people can 'verbalise' their thinking, they can 'visualise' it. The elements in an image represent concepts in a spatial context, rather than the linear form used for words. Speech and visual communication are parallel and usually interdependent means by which humans exchange information. A diagram, a map, and a painting are all examples of uses of visual language. Its structural units include line, shape, colour, motion, texture, pattern, direction, orientation, scale, angle, space and proportion.

Visual thinking, just like verbal thinking, necessitates an understanding of the cultural context and the larger visual vocabulary of that contextual visual language. For example in the western world the colour blue in clothing is used for boys and colour pink for girls. However this is not followed in the eastern world. In some countries red stands for danger. However in China it stands for celebration. This colour example is just one instance of visual language differing culturally. The meaning of shadow is culturally determined as well. In fact it can be said that visual languages are as unique and distinct as verbal languages. Just as the collection of phonemes that make the word pronounced have a different meaning whether you speak English or French natively, so too does red or shadow have different meaning depending on the visual language you speak.

While there are similarities between the visual and verbal language, we must be clear that the two are distinct. Talking about visual ideas can be a nice way to begin a project. It can be useful in terms of devising the palette of lights used by a designer. But once the lights are being turned on and off, and cues recorded, the thinking must be wholly visual. The thinking must be at the visual/emotional level rather than the verbal/rational level or the effort will fail.

Without visual thinking, without putting words aside and allowing the mind to focus wholly on what it sees before it, the creation of visual art is impossible. To improve visual thinking drawings help. When drawing, words not only don't help, they hurt. One must turn off the verbal part of the brain and just look and see; if the line is correct move on to the next one. If it is wrong correct it. The right answer is in your mind's eye.

People whose work involves thought as opposed to talk do their best thinking without words, using 'non-verbal thought'. Thus the process of visualisation begins with visual thinking.

2.3.4 Preparation of the Copy: Copy Thinking / Styles of Copy Creation

A copywriter in order to prepare the copy has to necessarily go through the following process. In fact, this process has to be done before he puts his pen to paper.

First, he thoroughly studies the characteristics of the target market, to which the ad message is to be targeted at. He then makes a thorough study of the product to be advertised and very diligently searches for the main attraction and the subsidiary attraction, that is, the advantages and benefits of the product and service to be advertised. Once these two exercises are carried out, the copywriter has to undertake an analysis of the selling points and benefits that the product and services offer to the buyers. As a result of this analysis, he comes out with the Unique Selling Proposition (USP) to be presented by him in the advertising message. The USP is the specialty of the product. (The special feature of the product) around which the advertising theme is prepared. For example, the 'creamy' 'Dove' soap or the 'transparent' 'Pears' soap. However, the prospects are not interested only in the selling points of the product. They are interested in the want or need fulfilling capacity of the product.

Thus, the USP has to be much a selling point with a consumer benefit; for example, the 'creamy' 'Dove' soap that results in soft skin. This matching of selling point with consumer benefit has to be done in a unique way. Thus, getting an effective USP idea or theme and presenting it properly is the most crucial aspect of copywriting.

In addition to the USP concept, knowledge of the six stages in the 'hierarchy of effects' model of **Levidge** and **Steiner** is very relevant to copy formulation. There are six stages to this model, namely, awareness, knowledge, liking, preference, conviction, and purchase. Advertising has often been called salesmanship in print or broadcasting. Thus, the copywriter should constantly be guided by the various stages in the selling process so that he forms an effective copy that is capable of moving the customer from awareness and knowledge of the product to purchasing it.

Thus, the advertisement copy should provide information and facts about the product or service in the first two stages; he should then aim at changing the attitudes and feelings or directing the desire to buy the products. A copywriter should know which stages are relevant to a particular advertisement copy. Not all the advertisements require a detailed inclusion of all the six stages. Some advertisements and commercials accomplish their objectives with a very simple copy structure; for example, ads of soft drinks contain only the first and last part, that is, awareness creation and motivation to purchase; whereas advertisements of high technology capital equipment when introduced for the first time may require all the stages, that is, from awareness and knowledge to conviction and purchase.

Even though the thinking process to be undertaken remains the same for whichever media it is to be written, yet some peculiarities do pertain to the drafting of the advertisement copy for each media. Here, let us study how the copy for the different media is prepared.

(A) Copy for Outdoor Media

If the copy is to be prepared for the outdoor media, it will basically contain three elements, namely, text, illustration and slogan. In place of illustration, sometimes, brand name or trademark is also used. The advertisement is restricted only to these three elements from the angles of clarity, legibility and effectiveness.

The effectiveness of an advertisement for this media can be harnessed by using simple and clear block letters. Spacing and colour combinations used in lettering contribute a great deal towards the effectiveness of advertising. The use of bold colours and effective and time-tested combinations like black on yellow, green on white, red on white etc., should be used. Outdoor advertising is fundamentally an art medium, and hence, rests on artwork in addition to the words. The illustration used must be graphic, bold and dynamic, projecting a true image of the product that is visible even from a great distance. In outdoor advertising, colours are great attention getters.

While making a copy for the outdoor media, the following points are to be remembered:

1. It should be short. For a running reader, too many words will be of no use. Experience shows that the copy message must not be more than five to six words. This is considered as the safe limit that assures total reading, grasping and action orientation.

2. It should portray people. The theme of the copy is to be grasped at a glance. The copy contents must be reasoned out at a glance. The prospects usually show a keen interest in illustrations containing people, particularly, people in action. Thus, this media would do well to use illustrations of people.

3. It should use a single idea. As said earlier, the message has to be taken in at a glance. Hence, it is better to concentrate on one single idea.

4. It should be simple. The copy for this media should be such that people understand it without any undue taxing of the brain.

5. It should display the product and product name. The copy for this media should have either the product or its name displayed at the optical centre so that there is no chance of it being missed.

6. It should be visible using limited elements, and a wise colour combination ensures visibility.

In short, copy for outdoor media must be so designed as to attract attention at a glance. They should be brief and carry messages that are easy to understand, appeal emotionally and create an impact that guarantees action or response.

(B) Copy for Print Media

The most important copy element for print media is the 'headline' idea. If the headline idea fails to attract the prospect to the message and the product, the remaining parts of the advertisement are wasted. The advertisement copy may be a word, message or it may have pictures with a short message or a slogan. The words and pictures should be complementary to each other. However, since pictures get better attention than the words in the headline above or below the picture, we invariably have advertisements in print with pictures, sketches, and visual symbols. Moreover, a dramatic or provocative picture or photograph can effectively create an emotional or tragic scene, and thus, become a good grabber of the given prospect's attention. Many copywriters use both pictures and words to put across their creative ideas.

A perfectly worded headline can create the required excitement. Headlines may be in many forms. Thus, we may have headlines asking questions or issuing warning and appeals. We may also have a testimonial headline in which a celebrity is making a statement or a newsflash headline. There is no right or wrong length or form for an effective headline. Each headline must relate clearly and specifically to the intended audience and to the rest of the advertisement, highlighting the product features and its USP.

After the headline comes the subhead. If the headline has already rightly suggested, the product's value to the consumers, the job of the subhead is easier. Subheads should further carry the idea of the theme and should help the reader to have more knowledge of the product and services. The subheads generally expand upon the headline idea.

After the subhead, comes the body copy. It stimulates a liking and preference for a product. It systematically develops the benefits and promise offered by the product, explains logically and rationally the product features and product values, and gives convincing arguments in favour of and evidence in support of, the claims made about the superiority of the advertised product. In the body copy various emotional, rational or moral appeals are used to persuade a consumer to buy a particular brand.

At the end, comes the closing idea. This is as important to the print advertisement copy as close of sale is important to personal selling. Since an ad is a one-way communication, it should be closed with enough information and motivation for the buyer to act. There are various ways in which the closing idea can be put forward. For example, *"act now"*, *"visit our dealer"*, *"send enquiries immediately to"*, *"special festival discount"*, etc.

(C) Copy for Broadcasting Commercials

While drafting a copy for a broadcasting commercial, the following points as given by **Mr. J. D. Bruke** must be kept in mind:

1. **Keep the copy simple:** Because the time span for this commercial is short, the copy should be kept simple and only one central theme should be stressed. Simple words meant for the common man should be used.

2. **Emphasise the visual:** For a broadcasting commercial to be aired on an audiovisual media, the copywriter must constantly think visually and keep in mind the pictures first and, then, build in the words. This is because the viewers are first conscious of what they see and only then of what they hear.

3. **Make words and pictures work together:** The words and pictures should concentrate on the same thing, and should be beautifully coordinated together.

4. **Do not over-change the scene:** The change of scenes should flow in a logical sequence. Too many changes in scenes may confuse the viewers. Maximum three scenes are advisable in case of a ten-second idea. Even a single scene will do.

5. **Use minimum players:** The players can be principals and extras. Principals are the actors and the actresses with speaking roles or those who are seen full face on camera. Extras are non-speaking bit players who are commonly providing a background. From the point of view of economy, the copywriter should include a minimum number of principals as necessary for the effectiveness of the commercial.

6. **Do not waste the opening:** The first few moments are of vital importance where it is a must to capture the attention and involvement of the viewer. This can be done by making startling statements, use of humour, conflict between two individuals etc. The opening scene must relate to the main theme of the idea.

7. **Follow through after the opening:** After a good opening, the rest of the copy should follow through effectively in a proper sequence. In making this sequence a success, the copywriter should avoid big, difficult and unusual words because the time is short and the viewer's interest is fleeting.

Thus, even though the copywriter writes the copy for the advertisements to be released in the various media, each media has its specialities and the copywriter should keep this in mind.

2.3.5 A.I.D.A. Formula (Attention: Interest: Desire: Action) / Approaches to Copy Creation

The design and development of advertising follows the AIDA formula.

The effectiveness of advertising depends upon to what extent the advertising message is received and accepted by the target audience. Research has identified that an advertisement to be effective has to (i) attract attention (ii) secure interest (iii) build desire for the product, and finally (iv) obtain action. All advertisements obviously do not succeed on these counts, and that is the one basic reason why there is a great difference between the number of people exposed to the advertisement and those who ultimately take the purchase decision. At the final stage of action, however, the other elements of the marketing mix, especially, distribution are crucial.

Advertisement communicates an idea, a message or a belief. An advertisement would be effective only if the media audience accepts that message and is motivated to take the required action. Several models have been developed which have specifically identified the sequence of events which must take place between receipt of the message and the desired action.

AIDA Model: A somewhat simplified model based on the identical principle of sequential stages of consumer action is known as AIDA model.

AIDA stands for:

- A – Attracting Interest
- I – Rousing Interest
- D – Building Desire
- A – Obtaining Action

Advertising as a communication medium can in most cases effectively perform the first three functions. In the case of direct action advertising, it also must translate desire into action, unaided by any other promotional instruments. In the case of indirect action advertising, however, the action can be aided at the time of purchase by a two-way communication between the intending buyer and the sales staff.

Let us examine the attention, interest, desire and action components in more detail.

1. **Attention:** The layout is the most important factor that directs attention to an advertisement. Typography and colours used in the layout can rivet us. The size of the advertisement also compels us to get attracted to it. Contrast by white space is a good attention getter. Movement is a vital element for getting the attention. Movement can be physical or emotional. The position and content of the headline are also important factors. The position of the advertisement itself adds to its attention value. Celebrities in the advertisement, dramatisation, model selection, and illustration all contribute to this attention.

2. **Interest:** Advertisement seen does not mean advertisement read. Mostly, people see the illustrations and headline and do not read the copy. Here, illustrations have to work hard. They should together with the headline provoke further reading. Thus, the selection of the illustration and its integration with real life is very important. Even copy format is important for interest creation. Some people get worked up by a scientific copy and, some others, by the humorous copy. Here, there is a dilemma for a copywriter. He has to satisfy maximum number of people so he has to work out some common factor of interest.

3. **Desire:** The basic purpose of advertising is to create a desire for the product or service being advertised. It is a function of appeals used for the motivation of people. Here, vivid description or copy always helps. Buying motives, physiological as well as psychological, make people purchase products. The copy of the advertisement must kindle these motives. There are certain barriers here: certain reservations in the minds of the customers. We have to overcome them. We have to convince by giving evidence, testimonials, endorsements, facts and figures. On arousal, people become prone to buy the product.

4. **Action:** The logical end to arousal of desire is the purchase action. Once an intense desire is created for the product, and if this is done by a direct action advertisement, it results in an immediate action. However, if desire is created by an indirect action advertisement, it will result in a favourable change in the attitude of the prospect that will lead to a future purchase action.

2.3.6 Pre-Testing Methods and Measurements

This topic has been dealt with in the first chapter under the heading effectiveness of advertising.

Points to Remember

*   An advertising copy is all the written or spoken matter in an advertisement expressed in words or sentences and figures designed to convey the desired message to the target consumers.

*   An institutional copy is one whose main aim is to build up a reputation for the selling house or its departments.

*   A human interest copy appeals to the emotions and the senses rather than the intellect and judgement.

*   A humorous copy fully exploits the sense of humour. This copy elicits fun, mirth and laughter.

*   A fear copy appeals to the sense of fear and arouses a keen interest in protecting our life and property from the source of fear.

- A predicament copy usually overlaps the other three kinds of human interest copies.

- A copy that is designed to educate the prospect is known as an educational copy.

- A suggestive copy tries to suggest or pinpoint or convey the message of the advertiser to the readers.

- In Scientific copy, the technical specifications of a product are explained.

- When the copy is integrated to a recent happening or event, it is said to be a topical copy.

- In Endorsement/Testimonial copies, a product is endorsed by an opinion leader who has a large following.

- The layout is the format in which the various elements of the advertisement are combined. The layout is thus a visual representation of the ideas of the creator of the advertisement.

- **'Trademark'** is a word, symbol or a device used to identify a manufacturer, goods or services and distinguishes them from those of others.

Questions for Discussion

1. What is advertising copy? Discuss its objectives and elements.
2. Explain the features and types of advertising copy.
3. What are the principles and components?
4. Elaborate the visualization and format of advertising layout.
5. Describe the approaches, principles and styles of copy creation.
6. Discuss the pre-testing methods and measurements of advertising copy.

■■■

Chapter **3**...

Media Decisions

Contents ...

Learning Objectives ...

- To understand the meaning and Functions of Advertising Media
- To Study the importance and process of Media Research
- To analyse the basics of Reach, frequency and continuity in Media Planning
- To know the various approaches of Media Selection
- To elaborate the types of Media

3.1 Advertising Media

3.1.1 Meaning and Definition of Advertising Media

The term media is plural for medium. In advertising terms medium is a channel of communication such as newspapers, magazines, radio and television. A medium is a vehicle for carrying the sales message of an advertiser to the prospects. It is a vehicle by which advertisers convey their messages to a large group of prospects and thereby aid in closing the gap between the producer at one end and the consumer on the other.

Advertising media may be defined as "the physical means whereby a manufacturer of goods or utilities or a supplier of services tells the consumer about his product or service".

In the words of **Brennan**, *"The term media embraces each and every method that the advertiser has at his command to carry his message to the public"*.

Thus, advertising media is a vehicle or device that carries the message of the advertiser to the target consumer. There are various media that are available for an advertiser to choose from to carry his particular advertising message. Here, let us discuss the various available media of advertising, their characteristics, advantages and disadvantages.

3.1.2 Functions of Advertising Media

The advertising media is nothing but a vehicle that carries the message of the advertiser to the consumer. Thus, the advertising media performs the function of carrying the message. As such the advertiser should ensure that the choice of media is such that the advertiser's message is effectively carried and conveyed in the right form and spirit as was meant by the advertiser. Further, the advertiser should choose such a media that enables the advertisement to discharge the function for which it was created. An advertisement broadly performs the following functions. Information function, precipitation function, persuasive function, re-enforcement function, reminder function and value adding function. All these have been discussed in chapter 1.

3.1.3 Types of Media

Advertising media can be classified into the following four groups.

(A) Indoor Advertising Media

1. Press media
2. Radio media
3. Television media
4. Film media
5. Internet/ Digital Media

(B) Outdoor Advertising Media

1. Posters
2. Painted displays
3. Travelling displays
4. Electric signs
5. Sky-writing
6. Sandwich-men

(C) Direct Advertising Media

1. Post cards
2. Envelope enclosures
3. Broad-sides
4. Booklets and catalogues
5. Sales letters
6. Gift novelties
7. Store publications
8. Package inserts

(D) Display Advertising Media

1. Displays
2. Showrooms
3. Exhibitions

Let us now study the characteristics, advantages and disadvantages of each advertising media.

(A) Indoor Advertising Media

Indoor advertising means those media that reach the audience right inside their houses or indoors. These vehicles are newspapers, radios, televisions and films. Through these media the message reaches the audience indoors where it is cosy and the audience is in a comfortable and receptive mood. The audience is relaxed. Let us study each of the indoor media.

1. Press Media or Print Media

Press or print media basically includes newspapers and magazines. Let us first consider newspaper media.

(i) **Newspapers:** It is very hard to imagine a morning without a newspaper. Millions of people all over the world begin their mornings with a cup of tea and the newspaper. The newspaper is not just the carrier of news but also ideas, opinions, complaints and thoughts of the people. It enlightens as well as entertains. Of all the media it is considered as the backbone of the advertising programme. This is because it has continued to remain the most powerful message carrier.

Merits of Newspaper Media

(a) **Local coverage:** Since newspapers are local, the advertisers can easily use them to reach a particular local market. Most newspapers contain maximum number of local advertisements. This is one of the major advantages as newspapers provide advertising in a geographically segmented market.

(b) **Lengthy and complex messages:** As newspapers can be scanned at the leisure of the reader, lengthy and complex messages can be released through this media.

(c) **It is comparatively cheap:** As compared to other media of advertising like television it is a cheaper media.

(d) **Ease of release:** It is very easy to release an advertisement in the newspaper. A previously prepared advertisement can be released at the last minute to take advantage of some special marketing situation.

(e) **Wide reach:** Newspapers have a wide reach as they are read by virtually everybody. It reaches even the remotest corners of the country.

(f) **Trial advertisements:** This media is good to conduct a trial advertisement run. This trial advertisement can be conducted on a small scale and on a regional basis at a relatively low cost.

Demerits of Newspaper Media

(a) **Short lifespan:** The biggest demerit of newspaper advertising is its short lifespan. Today's newspaper is tomorrow's wastepaper.

(b) **Chances of being unnoticed:** Newspapers are read basically to catch up on news and views. They are read in a hurry and readers tend to skip advertisements. Thus, an advertisement may go unnoticed if it is not strategically located.

(c) **Different rates:** Newspapers charge different rates for advertisements placed in different positions. The preferred positions often carry a higher rate. A majority of the newspaper advertisements are placed on an ROP basis, which means that the paper has the right to place the advertisement anywhere at its discretion. ROP means run of paper. Thus, the advertisement may get placed in a position which is not very eye-catching.

(d) **Poor Quality:** Newspapers are printed on coarse wood pulp paper known as newsprint. The quality of newspaper advertising is thus poor as compared to magazine advertising.

(ii) Magazines

Magazines are periodicals that are published weekly, fortnightly, monthly, quarterly and annually. Magazines are both specific interest magazines as well as general interest magazines. Further you also have both regional as well as national magazines.

Merits of Magazine Advertising

(a) **Longer life:** Magazines have a longer life as compared to newspapers. Further magazines are read at leisure and hence the advertisements have more chance of being noticed.

(b) **Visual display:** Magazines use good quality paper with a glossy finish. Further magazine advertisements have the advantage of colour and this makes them more visually appealing.

(c) **Selectivity:** As magazines usually have selective readership, a high degree of selectivity is provided to the advertiser through the use of this media. Advertisers can reach any market segment in terms of differing demographic variables like age, income, occupation, profession, sex and so on. It should also be noted that, magazines have a high degree of believability, acceptance and authority in their respective fields.

(d) **Geographical flexibility:** Magazines have regional editions through which the advertiser can reach an audience in a particular geographical area. Thus, the advertisement message can be tailor-made to suit the culture, language and outlook of a particular kind of people.

Demerits of magazine advertising

(a) **Inflexibility:** Advertisements to be released in magazines have to be submitted well in advance. In the case of some weekly magazines the space has to be bought and the advertisement copy submitted at least 8-10 weeks in advance, particularly in the case of colour advertisements. Once this date is over no changes in the advertisement copy is allowed nor can the space bought be cancelled.

(b) **Waste in circulation:** Though magazines have regional editions most of them have a national circulation. Thus, an advertisement that is released in a national magazine lacks geographical selectivity.

(c) **Costlier:** Advertisements in magazines are more costly than newspaper advertisements. This is because of the use of better quality paper, use of colours and mechanical preparations for advertisements.

(d) **Restricted Frequency:** As magazines are usually published weekly, fortnightly, monthly, quarterly or annually the advertiser cannot communicate his message to the audience with any high degree of frequency. Magazines are "occasional ambassadors" that eat away frequency and immediacy.

2. Radio Media

Radio advertising can aptly be called as "word of mouth" advertising. It is a medium of mass communication that appeals to the ears through sound. It is a media that is virtually dead or dying in the urban areas. However, about 37 percent of the rural population still get their information from the radio. Thus, it is an important media if the advertiser wants to reach the rural masses.

Merits of Radio Media

(a) **Selectivity:** Radio is a selective vehicle of mass media in the sense that the advertiser can advertise in only those markets that he desires. He can select programmes, stations, time of the day and the type of listenership.

(b) **Instant medium that is flexible:** Radio is an instant medium, in the sense it does not require the paraphernalia of camera and other things that is required for preparing television advertisements. In fact last minute alterations too can be easily done.

(c) **Human touch:** The human voice is the most natural way in which people communicate. Radio communication uses the human voice and thus it is a personal medium that gives a human touch.

(d) **Mass coverage:** Radio reaches almost all human beings except those that cannot hear. Further, it is a mobile medium. It can easily be carried along and hence, can be heard anywhere and at any time, easily and comfortably.

(e) **Economy:** Radio advertising is cheaper as compared to other media like television or even prime hoardings.

Demerits of Radio Advertising

(a) **Lack of illustration:** Radio is one medium in which it is virtually impossible to show or even illustrate a product. The only way in which the product can be shown through this medium is through an oral description.

(b) **Message perishability:** Usually a person who listens to the radio does not do so with complete attention. In fact, work or play is usually undertaken and the radio makes up the background sound. In such a situation the advertisement message may go unheard and perish away without any effective listening.

(c) **Limited time:** The time available for advertising is limited to a specific number of hours only. Once this time is sold, no more advertisements can be accommodated. This is not the case with the print media where extra pages can be added.

3. Television

In India the television was first commissioned in 1959 and commercial telecasting started only in 1976. It is an audio visual medium that provides a perfect synchronisation of sound, light, motion, colour and immediacy.

Merits of Television Advertising

(a) **It has a deep impact:** No other medium can compete with the television as far as effective presentation is concerned. It attracts attention immediately. Computer graphics have made it more effective than ever before. Through this medium the product is shown exactly as it is. It can be demonstrated. In fact it virtually replaces personal selling.

(b) **Mass communication media:** Like the radio, television too is a media of mass communication. Nearly the entire urban area and a great portion of rural India too enjoy television coverage. Every slum area in an urban town boasts of a television. The poorest of the poor aspire for it. Thus, it reaches a maximum number of people every day in their houses.

(c) **Upper hand in distribution:** A television advertisement for a product or service is greatly appreciated by the merchants in the channel of distribution. They attach a certain amount of prestige towards handling products that are advertised on television. Thus, this medium helps the marketer in procuring the best distributors for distributing his products.

(d) **Lifelike presentation:** The most striking feature of television medium is its instantaneous transmission of sight, motion, sound and colour that is lifelike. Of all the media, television is the closest replica of life. It presents the things and the events as they are and happen. Thus, it is the most believable medium. People tend to believe what they see.

(e) **Evocation of experience:** It stimulates the experience of using and owning the product, thus creating a desire for it.

(f) **Image building:** Television succeeds in building a powerful image of the company and its products. It can also project an image of the users rendering it excellent for lifestyle advertising.

Demerits of Television Advertising

(a) **It is time consuming:** It takes time to produce television commercials. This medium requires planning and deliberation. If it is not properly produced the television commercial may look crude. But once produced as per requirement they can be repeated over a long period of time.

(b) **Short life:** The television commercial has a short life. Once it is viewed and heard it is gone. It does not remain as a part of the household like the newspaper or magazine or the calendar. If the prospect misses the commercial at its exact time of presentation, the scene and message is lost and wasted as far as the prospect is concerned. It requires a repeated relay of advertisements to have an appreciable impact on the audience.

(c) **A costly medium:** Television is a costly medium. Not only is it costly to make a television advertisement, but the purchase of time on the television is also very expensive. This is one of the main factors that take television out of the reach of the small advertiser. He cannot even think of purchasing a slot on television.

(d) **The clutter problem:** Television media suffers from the clutter problem. That is over crowding of too many commercials in a very short span of time. Both the advertisers and the viewers complain about this. The clutter reduces the effectiveness of the advertisements.

(e) **An immobile medium:** The television is an immobile medium. Radio can be listened to either in the car or while walking, on a picnic etc. Similarly, newspapers and magazines are read everywhere. However, television is viewed only at home.

4. **Film Advertising Media**

Film advertising is yet another medium of publicity characterised by sound, motion, colour, vision and timeliness. It is like a television run on an enlarged screen for a larger audience. This audio-visual medium has a wide range starting from an ordinary slide presentation to the screening of advertising films. Screen advertisements are liked by people of all ages, sexes, professions, political affiliations, cultural heritages and income groups because of the magic of life-size presentation of themes.

Merits of Film Advertising

(a) **Film advertising ensures a captive audience:** People visit a cinema hall to see a movie of their choice. This choice ensures a higher degree of concentration as compared to viewing a television programme. Television cannot command complete attention as commanded by the film media.

(b) **Film media is ideal for niche marketing:** Through this media the advertiser can be segment specific, market specific right down to a particular district, city or even a theatre.

(c) **Advertising in cinema is economical:** The cost of screening an advertisement in a theatre is quite economical. However, the cost of making an advertising film is not so.

Demerits of Film Advertising

(a) **It is costly:** The cost of making an advertising film to be screened in cinema houses is expensive. However, the cost of making slides is not so.

(b) **Limited coverage:** The coverage of film advertising is only limited to those few who visit the cinema hall in which these advertisements are released.

(c) **Resentment from viewers:** The viewers go to cinema houses for viewing a feature film and not an advertising film. The viewers view the advertisements to be a barrier in their entertainment and may resent it. This reduces the effectiveness of the advertisement message.

5. Internet/ Digital Advertising:

The Internet is one of the latest media of advertising. It has a worldwide reach. People all over the world can access the Internet. When a person accesses a particular web page, the advertisements released on that particular web page are also viewed by him. Thus the more popular a particular web page the more in demand it is by advertisers. This is the reason why many a services are available for free on the Internet. When the services are free the viewer ship is more and this increased accessing of a particular site attracts advertisers.

(B) Outdoor Advertising Media

Outdoor advertising is the oldest form of advertising. It is also known as 'position', 'mural' or 'indirect' advertising. Outdoor advertising is literally outdoor, that is, it is out of the home or place of business. The importance of outdoor advertising can be gleaned from the fact that an ordinary human being spends one third of his time outdoors. The viewer has to incur no expenditure, nor has he to make any effort of see an outdoor advertisement. An outdoor advertising message is not bought to the viewer; it is the viewer who goes to the message, though they view it in the course of their other activities. Outdoor advertising media is made up of posters, painted displays, hoardings, electric signs, travelling displays, skywriting, and the like. A detailed explanation of various outdoor media means is as follows:

1. **Posters:** A poster is a sheet of paper pasted on a wooden, card or metal board depicting the advertising message. The poster advertising message should be simple, brief and attractive. Illustrations go a long way in increasing the effectiveness of posters. Mostly posters remain in position for a period of time, say several weeks. We therefore, say that they enjoy 24 hours exposure and a long life. Posters account for nearly 75 percent of all outdoor media means. The success of a poster advertisement depends upon the designing of the poster as well as the site at which it is put up.

2. **Painted Displays:** Painted displays are painted bulletins and wall paintings. A painted bulletin is nothing but a metal sheet of a rectangular shape of a standard size erected at heights to command visibility from a distance. It is a larger and elaborate form of outdoor advertising as compared to the poster. Painted displays are sometimes illuminated for night traffic. The rentals for these sites are based on a period of one year. The advertiser may thus keep the same message for a period of one year or change it depending upon his requirement.

3. **Electric Signs/Neon Signs:** Electric signs and neon signs are more popularly known as spectacular signs. These are large permanent signs that make use of elaborate light and action effects. These are a conspicuous means of outdoor media and are designed to attract the public as they pass by. They are usually effective in places that have a high nightlife. Electric signs are usually placed in high places so as to have a maximum rate of visibility. These signs are either authorised by the local administration or are put up on private buildings. Usually these signs are on a yearly contract.

4. **Travelling Displays/Transit Advertising:** Transit advertising stands for all types of advertising signs or displays used in trains, buses, cars, trams, autos and other such transportation vehicles and the terminals or the stations from which they operate.

5. **Skywriting:** The advertising industry has very creatively used the sky to advertise their goods and services. Skywriting is the kind of publicity where the message is spread across the sky in one form or the other. Usually skywriting takes the form of sky balloons, giant kites, and search lights. This is a novel medium and can catch the attention of the people. However, it has a short life, and is not very commonly used.

6. **Sandwichmen:** This is the oldest and funniest medium of outdoor advertising. It is still popular in rural areas. Under this kind of advertising, the advertiser hires men, known as 'sandwichmen' because they are sandwiched between the posters both in the front and back. Further they are dressed in colourful and bright clothes, and shout slogans, thus attracting the public not just towards themselves but to the product and the advertiser.

Merits of Outdoor Media

(a) The outdoor media offers longevity.

(b) It offers geographic selectivity. Posters can be changed as often as required to keep up with the change in the advertising message to suit a particular segment in the market. This is one medium in which the advertiser has a choice of displaying a different message in every region and every locality.

(c) The advertiser can incorporate the names and addresses of his local dealers or agents at the bottom of the poster or painted display. These dealer imprint strips are called 'snipes'.

(d) This media offers an attractive display of the product trademark and slogan.

(e) This media attracts the attention of the people when they are outdoors. Thus, it results in influencing them when they are out shopping. Usually these posters and painted displays are strategically placed so as to have maximum effect.

Demerits of Outdoor Media

(a) Since the copy of this media has to be brief, this media merely supplements some other media.

(b) This media is non-selective, in the sense that the audience who get the exposure are people of all ages, sexes, educational and socio-economic levels. There is no selectivity of a particular type of audience.

(c) This media when employed on a national basis is relatively expensive.

(d) It is difficult to measure the effectiveness of this media and getting reliable data on the number of people who actually see these advertisements, and is very difficult to estimate.

(C) Direct Advertising Media

There is a lot of confusion between the phrase 'direct advertising' and 'direct mail advertising'. Direct advertising is a very comprehensive phrase covering all forms of printed advertising delivered directly to the prospective customer. Instead of using an indirect media like newspaper or television through which the prospect may or may not see the advertisement, through this media the prospect is directly approached. It may take various forms like pamphlets distributed to people on the road, stuck under the windscreen of an automobile, handed over at the retail counter or it may be sent through post. It is 'direct mail advertising' only if it reaches the customer through the post. However, if it reaches the customer in any other way it is 'direct advertising'. This is one of the oldest ways of reaching a prospect or customer. It is a direct approach to consumers. This direct approach may be through sales letters and circulars, or it may be through leaflets, folders and brochures.

The following are the different forms that a direct advertising can take:

1. **Post Cards:** A post card is the most widely used form of direct advertising because of its high attention value and economy. It is designed to get direct and immediate attention of the recipient. It is used to carry brief messages.

2. **Envelope Enclosures:** The phrase 'envelope enclosure' is quite likely to mislead. By 'enclosure', we normally mean a paper that is enclosed or attached to the main letter. However, here it stands for the bunch of papers itself which is separately posted. It may be a circular, a 'stuffer' or a folder.

    A 'circular' is a sheet of paper or sheets of papers printed on either one or both sides. A circular gives information about the product in colour or in black and white. They may or may not carry illustrations of the product

    A 'stuffer' is an enclosure that is used as a means to deliver sales and goodwill messages. It is a means used to amplify the sales literature by providing illustrations and detailed information of a wide range of commodities of a single company or different manufacturers.

    A 'folder' is bigger than an ordinary card or a letter. It is folded in an impressive and convenient manner. It is very popularly known as adult leaflet or booklet without binding.

3. **Board Sides:** Board side is a large size advertising folder. Its striking features are its big size and illustrative display. These are also called as 'spectaculars in print' because they are excellent attention getters.

4. **Booklets and Catalogues:** Booklets are very small books consisting of not more than 8-10 pages fastened or stapled together to allow it to open like a book. A booklet is usually mailed in an envelope. It contains useful information answering the questions of prospective buyers about product features. However, it gives information about a limited number of products. Catalogues are quite similar to the booklet in physical make-up. However, they are much larger and present information on a wide range of

products of the business house. They also feature the prices of the products and give other conditions of purchase. They can be used as reference material too.

5. **Sales Letters:** A sales letter is a silent ambassador of the firm. It first sells the name of the company and then its products. The success of a sales letter depends upon its appeal. The stationery used, the tone of the letter, the theme of the letter, all have their impact.

6. **Gift novelties:** Gift advertising or specialty advertising is the medium that employs useful articles known as advertising specialities or gift novelties that are imprinted with the name and address and the sales message of the advertiser. These act as goodwill gifts or reminders. The advertiser hopes that the recipient is likely to be influenced favourably to buy in the future, if he is reminded of the company every time he looks at the gift. There are countless such items that can be presented like ballpoint pens, ashtrays, cigarette lighters, paperweights, calendars, drink stirrers etc.

7. **Store Publications:** A store publication is a house organ or bulletin or magazine or miscellany published by the company mainly for the purpose of promoting goodwill and moulding the public opinion, though it has a sales tinge. These house organs are freely distributed to the dealers, customers, and employees. Though they are costly and have a high mortality rate, a well-edited house organ can do a lot in getting customers, and dealers acquainted with the company's image, philosophy and progress.

8. **Package Inserts:** The phrase 'package inserts' is used in a broad sense to include packages, labels, and inserts. Though the package is a container that protects the contents and facilitates easy handling, it is a very effective means of carrying the message about the product. It acts as a medium of advertising. For better results, the advertising message on the package must be short, illustrative and giving product information and uses. 'Label' is a printed piece of paper giving the value of the product and its content, name of the product and producers and other such useful information. It is stuck or imprinted on the package. 'Package inserts' are printed matter that is inserted into the packages. They go only to those who purchase the particular product. They provide a golden opportunity to the advertiser to pass on his message to the customers. Inserts give information regarding how best to use the product, as well as how to store and maintain it. This is also the most economical method of direct advertising.

Merits of Direct Advertising Media

(a) **High selectivity:** Through the use of this media, the advertiser can select exactly which particular target audience he wishes to reach out to.

(b) **Personal touch:** This media allows for a personal touch, especially sales letters. They can be directly addressed to the particular person.

(c) **Deep impact:** The recipient receives these mailers at home, in a comfortable atmosphere. Further, if they are addressed to him personally, they will have a deeper impact.

(d) **Measurement of effectiveness:** This is the only media in which some kind of definite measurement of the effectiveness of the message can be done. Depending upon the response received, the effectiveness of the advertising message can be measured.

Demerits of Direct Advertising Media:

(a) **Higher cost:** The cost per recipient works out to be much more than other mass media like newspapers, magazines, radio and television.

(b) **Low reader interest:** Much of the material sent through direct advertising finds itself in the dustbin.

(c) **Warrants special skill:** To be effective this media needs to be prepared very creatively. It has to attract the attention of the reader and hence requires special talents.

(D) Display Advertising Media

Display advertising media, in a broader sense is also known as POP, that is, point-of-purchase advertising. It is more a promotional medium than advertising. In recent times this medium is gaining more importance because of new trends in buying such as 'self-service'. The significance of display advertising lies in its ability to allow the prospects to experience the products before buying. It is also an effective dealer aid. It attracts customers to the shop and leads to impulse buying.

Display advertising is hinged on the concept of display. It has three dimensions namely displays, showrooms and showcases, and exhibitions. Let us take a brief look at all of these.

1. **Displays:** Displays are of several types. There are window displays, counter displays, wall displays, shelf displays, overhead displays, floor displays, and jumble displays. Here, let us study the prominent ones namely window display and counter display.

    Window display: The "display" of products in shop windows so that passersby are attracted to enter the shop and buy the products, or at least be reminded of the products, is termed as "window display". Window display is an effective strategy for gaining the interests and attention of the passersby or 'window shoppers'. Attractive and innovative window displays attract and urge window shoppers to step into the shop. Today, the concept of window display has caught on so well in India that a new breed of designers specialising in the art of window display has emerged.

    Counter display: Counter display or interior display refers to all the arrangements that are made inside the shop. It refers to all kinds of internal showmanship in the garb of storage. It can be open, closed, top-of-the-counter, wall, architectural, ledge type and the like. It speaks of scientific and artistic arrangement of glass cupboards, fixtures, shelves, racks, showcases, stands and other supports.

2. **Showrooms:** Even today there are some customers who do not believe in purchase without inspection. In the case of industrial goods and consumer goods purchase after inspection is inevitable. Sometimes, demonstrations are also required prior to purchase. Showrooms basically accommodate the needs of such consumers.   A showroom is a specially designed room used mainly for display, demonstration and after sale services with two types of personnel, namely technical and sales staff. A showroom becomes the hub of activity of explaining the product features, merits, demonstrating and after sale services, particularly repairs and maintenance.

3. **Trade shows, exhibitions and fairs:** Trade shows and exhibitions offer an excellent opportunity to manufacturers to display their products and to demonstrate their use and value. Manufacturers can buy display spaces or counters at reasonable rates, perhaps more reasonable than the exorbitant media rates for advertising. Many a times, trade associations too hold annual exhibitions and fairs. Nowadays electronic fairs, technology fairs, consumer products exhibitions have become quite common.

Thus, the above are the various media that are available for an advertiser to choose from in order to advertise his products. He may choose any combination of the various media mentioned above. However, his choice of selection of media is affected by the following factors. Let us take a look at these.

3.2 Media Planning

3.2.1 Meaning

Media planning is a general term and encompasses all decisions regarding not only the selection of media but also decisions regarding the time and place of advertising. A 'Media Plan' thus outlines how advertising time and space in various media will be used to achieve the marketing objectives of the company through advertising. 'Media Planning' thus involves not only 'media selection', but also the drawing up of an advertising schedule.

3.2.2 Importance of Media Planning

The Importance of advertisement and promotion is being recognised by the companies these days and therefore companies have started to go in for Media Planning of advertisements and promotions so as to achieve better sales and hence better profits. Media planning refers to the best possible method to get the advertiser's message across to the target market. The main objective of media plan is to find the perfect combination of media vehicles that shall enable the message to be communicated to the larger chunk of the buyers.

3.2.3 Media Planning Process

The following are the steps to be followed in designing a Media Plan.

1. **Study of the Target Market/Target Market study**

The first step in media planning is the gathering of useful data about the target market or audience to be reached through advertising. The more detailed and specific the data available on the target market, the more appropriate will be the selection of the media. The advertiser must have a full understanding of the target market. For an appropriate media plan, it is essential to know the type or class of consumers — whether all types are women, children, old people, etc. They may be professional people, businessmen, farmers, working class people, etc. The kind of data required about the target audience can be classified as follows: (This information is available from consumer research studies).

- **Demographic Data:** Is a population data regarding age, sex, income, religion, language etc., of the target audience.

- **Psychographic Data:** Is a 'psychological' data about the lifestyles of the various segments of the population, their varied cultures, beliefs and tastes.

- **Consumer Profile:** Is the tastes and preferences of the target audience with reference to different products, and, in particular, to the specific product or brand that is to be advertised.

- **Media Profile:** Is the media habits and preferences of the target market/audience. Newspapers, magazines, radio, television and other media, each has a different coverage. National dailies have different readership from the local or regional readers. This is equally true of magazines. There are sports magazines, business as well as film magazines, each have their own following. Similarly, the radio and television have their own audience. Different radio and television channels as well as programmes have a different following.

2. **Deciding the Advertising Message/Copy Formulation**

The second significant step in media planning is to decide upon the nature of the message to be conveyed to the target market. However, this decision can be taken only after the target audience/consumer profile has been understood perfectly. The message or the copy is decided in the light of the consumer behaviour or motivation that is intended to be influenced. The copy of an advertisement also depends upon the type of media in which it is to be released. Only an appropriate media can give a proper expression to the advertisement message and create a lasting impression on the minds of consumers. Newspapers may carry advertisements only in black and white, whereas magazines may express the copy in colour. The magic of colour in effectively attracting the attention to the ad message is well-known. It is found that orange, red and blue stand high on the attention getting list of colours. Men prefer orange, while women like red. These preferences for colour are useful and significant. In fact, colour is an important means of creating an emotional feeling around an advertisement, and around a product advertised. Similarly, some photographs and actions in advertisements are more effective if expressed in colour. Some advertisements need only to be announced on radio there is no need of visual, photo or action.

When the same product is advertised on the radio, the message is put in such a way that it goes down effectively with listeners. Sometimes, messages are presented in a lyrical form, which is pleasant to the ears. But when the same product is advertised in, say a magazine, the audience reads the copy of the advertisement; and it should, therefore, be an eye catcher. While reading an advertisement we have more time to think and analyse it objectively. When the same product is advertised on television, the audience has the opportunity of viewing it in addition to listening to it. The copy in such a case has to be different from the copy in the other two media. Thus, in this stages the copy is formulated keeping in mind the consumer and the media.

3. The marketing media and the target group

Once the target audience has been analysed and the copy is ready, the next step is to search for the right media keeping in mind the media profile of the audience. For example, if the target audience is the youth, then, that media should be chosen that has reach vis-a-vis the youth. However, while choosing the media, various other considerations like cost, product prestige, rival brands advertising media etc., should be kept in mind. Further, at this stage it, is also necessary to give some thought to which media will match the copy perfectly. Sometimes, the copy is so made that it matches only with the audio video media. In such a case, the choice of media available for selection is reduced.

4. Media Selection

The fourth and final step in media planning is deciding the media vehicle or vehicles based on the reach, the frequency and the size of the advertising budget. The 'media vehicle' may be an individual newspaper or magazine or radio programme or T.V. serial or video film to be used for exposing the advertisement.

Reach is expressed in terms of the number of households or individuals covered by a given medium over a period of time. This is usually expressed in terms of percentage of total households or individuals in the target market. Sometimes, there is a possibility of duplication, that is, the target audience may be reached by two media. National magazines have a different reach from that of the regional ones or other media, such as, T.V., radio, etc. National readership surveys provide information about published materials, whereas several other conducted studies may provide the reach per cent of other media.

Frequency refers to the average number of times different households or individuals are reached by a medium in a given period of time. The frequency of advertisement exposure of the target market depends upon the amount of reinforcement of the image required or the amount of reminding required to have a sustaining patronage from the target customers. The greater the frequency, the greater the probability of the advertisement message to make a lasting impression.

Media selection has to be based on the budget available. The concept of 'What can you afford?' is equally relevant to small as well as large companies. For large companies too have a budget or an allocation of fund for promotion. The baseline for choice of media boils down to how much money a company can afford to put in for a particular market for advertising and promotion.

The media to be selected also depends upon the type of the product and the characteristics of the distribution channel.

Type of Product: The type of product and services to be advertised also determines the media to be selected. Industrial products and new products of a technical nature are advertised through 'purchase' magazine. Products for exports are advertised in 'products from India' or the 'product finder'. Fashion-wear is advertised in film, general or fashion magazines like *Society, Stardust, Cosmopolitan*, etc.

New products when introduced should be supported with advertising in media that can give exposure of the product to the audience as sensational news with some degree of urgency. National or regional dailies, radio and television are appropriate, but not fortnightly or monthly magazines.

Advertisements for a product, with the objective of carving a market segment for it and creating a strong brand loyalty by a conscious attempt at giving the product a personality are liked by the consumers of this segment. This necessitates the designing of advertisements highlighting the various personality traits of the target user or the group. The copy design of the advertisement and the media through which the advertisement is released should have a similar personality if advertising is to be effective.

Characteristics of the Distribution channel: The media of advertising chosen also depends upon the distribution channel. Distribution outlets may be classified into national, regional and local. When advertising is done on a national basis, using adequate national media, the product should be made available nationally. When distribution is restricted to the regional level, advertising on the national basis would be mostly wasteful. In short, advertising would be of little or no value in getting the people to buy products unless these products are made available in an area that is within the easy reach of the consumers. Even when the product is nationally distributed, there are pockets or areas in which the company wants to operate more intensely. In such territories or regions, advertising may be more effective if done through regional magazines or dailies, which have greater readership than the national ones. Similar may be the case with the broadcasting media. In India, this is significantly true, for we have many regional languages.

When products are sold through a network of dealer and distributors who are few in number, though influential, advertising to such few target customers may be more effectively done through direct mail or trade journals. In short, the characteristics of distribution determine media selection.

Thus, media selection is the final stage in media planning.

3.2.4 Difficulties in Media Planning

In the huge gamut of media opportunities available, there are many challenges and difficulties in media planning. Media Planning is a process of detailed working of a huge number of elements in different permutations and combinations so as to achieve the best of results at the least of prices.

1. **Detailing and matching of Media with Marketing Objectives:** The first and foremost difficulty is around the contemplative phase where the media planner conducts a detailed appraisal of each medium and measures its advantages and disadvantages along with the attributes of the product and its marketing objectives. The best possible medium showing good level of agreement with the objectives of marketing and advertising is selected by the media planner as the brand communication tool.

2. **Lack of information:** Another challenge in media planning is the scarcity of information about the various market segments and target market. This lacuna of target market data makes the task of media planning even more intimidating and painstaking. The marketer has to start from 'ground zero' to research the target segment with little or no secondary data available.

3. **Inconsistent terms:** The next difficulty is in context with the discrepancies between the language and terms of internal strategic research team and the language and the terms of external media research. The larger the difference, the more difficult the task becomes for the marketer as his initial research findings were in proper synchronisation with the strategic intent of the company, which is obviously not incorporated by the mass media while they are showcasing their findings.

4. **Severe time pressure:** Another difficulty that the media planning team faces is that of time constraints and pressures. The media planning team has too much to do in a very limited time frame. They have to evaluate the various media vehicles available followed by evaluation of their pros and cons, then evaluation of the success of the product when a particular media vehicle is used, the cost factor also need to be considered, so basically a lot of work in a very short time frame is expected from the media planning team.

5. **Difficulty measuring effectiveness:** The effectiveness of the media planning is very difficult to measure as a lot of factors play a role in the success or downfall of an advertisement campaign. It is very difficult to trace the extent to which the media planning has been effective.

3.2.5 Basics of Reach, Frequency and Continuity in Media Planning

1. **Reach**

   Reach is simply the percentage of persons in a target population that is exposed to an advertising schedule at least once.

   In advertising, **'reach'** is defined as the size of the audience who listens to, reads, views or otherwise accesses a particular advertisement in a given time period. Reach may be stated either as an absolute number or, as a fraction of a given population (for instance, 'TV households', 'men' or 'those between the ages of 25-35).

   For any given viewer, they have been 'reached' by the advertisement/media if they have viewed it all (or a specified amount) during the specified time period. Multiple viewings by a single member of the audience in the cited time period does not increase reach.

   Since reach is a time-dependent summary of aggregate audience behaviour, reach figures are meaningless without a time period associated with them.

   Reach of television channels is often expressed in the form of x minute weekly reach - that is, the number (or percentage) of viewers who watched the channel for at least x minutes in a given week.

   For example, the reach of a television channel is the percentage of the population in private households who view a channel for more than x no. of minutes in a given day or week. Similarly, for radio, the weekly reach of a radio channel can be defined as the number of people who tune into a radio channel for at least x minutes in a given week

2. **Frequency**

   'Frequency' simply measures the number of times a person sees your message in a given advertising schedule. One person may see your commercial three times over your advertising flight. That would be a frequency of three.

   What are ratings, and how do they affect reach?

   A rating refers to the percentage of a target population that is actually watching a TV programme or listening to a radio station. For instance, if "Taarak Mehta ka Ooltah Chashmah" has a rating of 15.0, it means that fifteen percent of that target population is watching that particular programme.

   The rating for a TV/radio programme can also be called its reach. Using the same example of -"Taarak Mehta ka Ooltah Chashmah" - if its rating is 15.0, it reaches fifteen percent of the audience. When you add several groups of ratings together, for getting Gross Rating Points, or GRPs, you are then able to determine how much of our target audience we are reaching with the total number of GRPs in our schedule.

Ratings are important as they let the advertiser know exactly how good the response is to the advertisement. It lets him know what his investment in advertising is giving him. GRP's are important to the media too, as higher the GRP, the more the media can charge for its advertising time slots.

3. **Continuity**

Continuity is the Length of time that a media schedule will run it also takes into account whether it will be continuous or periodic. Continuity has a great importance because the advertisement retention capacity of the customers is incredibly short. The viewers/customers often forget the advertisement if it is not reinforced by frequent exposure. It would hence be inappropriate for a marketer to spend money on running an advertisement for one week which will be followed by another run after a gap of two to six months. Such long gaps will be unable to reinforce the advertising message

There are three types of continuity Patterns:

- **Continuous**: Spreading of the advertisement evenly throughout the campaign
- **Flighting:** Alternating between the periods of advertising and then eventually leading to no advertising
- **Pulsing:** Fluctuating the intensity of advertising throughout the campaign (a combination the two above)

Repetitive exposure to the message is needed to impact on the memories of consumers. As the repetition in the number of exposure increases, the number of people who remember it is bound to increase. The length of time for which the customers retain the message also increases. Message retention and recalling are the keys to succeed in media planning.

3.3 Media Research

3.3.1 Meaning of Media Research

Media research is an extremely important branch of marketing research. Publications (press, TV, radio) require a profile of their readership, what their readers are, where they are, how much they earn, what education they have, their media habits, their product habits, their life-style studies etc.   Media research in India has remained confined to NRS (National Readership Surveys). NRS is conducted generally for print media. In spite of extensive reach of TV, the press continues to receive lion's share of ad revenue everywhere. Apart from NRS, now we have TV and broadcast media viewership surveys. IMRB's and Television Rating Points (TRP) studies which convert the programmes viewership into percentages form the basis of TV advertising. We require a good deal of research into TV media.

The primary function of media research is to select the media most efficient for the advertisement campaign (media mix research). It is a pan of media planning. Here the research is concerned with what type of media should be used- Magazines?, Newspaper?, TV?, Outdoor? If magazines, of what classes?, General interest magazines, women's magazines, crime magazines, business magazines? If general interest magazines are to be used which specific ones — India Today, Sunday, Onlooker, Outlook? If newspapers, in which regions? If radio or TV, which coverage is in mind — national network or regional?

Once media selection is made based upon our research data regarding product, market, target audience, demographic and geographic and psychographic factors, the next logical step is to determine by research the combination or 'mix' of the media one must use to achieve the desired promotional objectives. Here, the media and the target market are to be matched. The over-riding factor is that of the ad budget. A balanced mix can be achieved by right type of research. It considers the research inputs of frequency and reach. Research guides us whether to use one type or varied media mix. Research also tells about the 'wear out' effect when the message is repeated and people become bored with it. We also know by research the media impact, for example, heavy watchers of TV are light readers of magazines, and vice versa. Concentration on TV ads alone will have greater impact on heavy viewers and very little impact on light viewers. The impact is uneven. It is to be balanced. Media mix research also covers the duplication effect, gross audience concept and media scheduling. These days complex mathematical models (like LP and simulation) are used in media mix research. There can be a problem of media measurement, the parameters of which are reach, frequency, yield per rupee and effectiveness. Out of this, effectiveness of media is very difficult to measure. The researchers are trying to develop one method to equal all parameters on different media.

3.3.2 Importance of Media Research

It has been observed that media research concerns itself with every phase of Media Selection activity. It covers a very wide area and is a tool that pervades every marketing activity. Its need and importance can be judged from the following discussions:

1. **Helps in Decision-Making:** Media research helps decision-making in regards to media selection etc. It provides a logical basis for decisions. Such decisions are based on concrete data, tests, experiments and expert opinions.

2. **Management Planning:** Media research is used for management planning. Marketing management can access the resources that can be useful for the business. Short and long term planning can be effectively formulated with the help of media research. The research inputs are helpful to managers planning new market programs and existing market expansion with relation to media decisions.

3. **Problem Solving:** Starting from problem identification to formulation of alternative solutions, and evaluating the alternatives in every area of marketing management, is

the problem solving action of media research. Problem solving media research focuses on the short range and long range decisions related to Media Selection. It can help management bring about prompt adjustment and innovations selection of media vehicle for the success of the advertisement campaign.

4. **Large Scale Production:** It helps the manufacturers in taking suitable decisions for large-scale production by exploiting the resources available in the most optimum manner. It helps to explore, identify and tap virgin markets to adopt intensive and extensive production techniques. Hence, it helps the management to bring about change in product designs, to meet the changing marketing needs.

5. **Formulation of Market Strategy:**   While formulating a new business plan the researcher can have market penetration strategy. In other words, he form can also think of developing new geographical market segments for current new geographic products. Media research helps us to determine market coverage strategies or positioning strategies.

6. **Media research Improves Marketing Efforts:** Media research makes one realise the type of media that has more chances of success or is having a potential demand. Pre-decided advertising Budget makes pricing easier and reasonable for the products. It enables the firm to offer these products to the right customers, which in turn improves sales performance and ultimately reduces the marketing costs.

7. **Employment Opportunities:** The increased production, widespread distribution and sales promotion activities increases the employment opportunities in the country. Hence it helps the unemployed people to get themselves gainfully employed in the diversified economic activities which are available because of media research.

8. **Increase in National Income:** With the increase of production distribution and marketing activities the national income increases. The increased national income helps to increase the per capita income, which ultimately increases the purchasing power of the consumers.

3.3.3 Functions of Media Research

Media Research is also called "Audience Research". It provides detailed information regarding the effectiveness and popularity of each advertising medium along with its comparative position of the cost of advertising in each medium. This facilitates the selection of the most suitable media mix that benefits the advertiser.

Media Research team carries out varied types of functions however the major functions it performs are:

1. **Vehicle Distribution:** This is a physical count of units through which advertising is distributed. It is the effect of media purely. Measurement techniques include newspaper and magazine circulation studies, TV ratings and radio-tuning studies, online media page requests and searches, and billboard locations.

2. **Vehicle Exposure:** This is a count of the number of people who are exposed to the media vehicle and those whose eyes or ears are open. This is also a pure media effect.

3. **Advertising Exposure:** This is a count of the number people exposed to the media vehicle and are also exposed to its advertising message. It is the highest level of measurement that is still a mostly pure media effect. Techniques of measurement include radio and TV commercial audience ratings, print ad page exposure studies, online ad view counts, billboard traffic counts etc.

3.3.4 Process of Media Research

The media research process is a five-step application of the scientific method.

The scientific method that includes

1.   Definition of the problem

2.   Situation analysis

3.   Obtaining problem-Specific data

4.   Interpretation of data

5.   Problem solution Step

Let's see them all one by one:

Step 1: Definition of the Problem: Defining the problem is most important and often the most difficult a step in the marketing research process. In this step, the objectives of the research must be clearly defined. The manager must think about what decisions need to be made and must clearly specify what information is really needed to make them. The manager and the researcher should both be involved so that both agree on the major objectives of the research. The problem definition step sounds simple but it is not so. A manager may assume that all of the questionable areas are obvious or that the researcher really understands what information is needed. However the important questions may be ignored while less important questions may be analysed in depth. It is also easy to fall into the trap of mistaking symptoms for the definition of the problem. Sometimes the research priorities are very clear, like a manager wants to know if the household he has targeted has tried a new product and what percentage of them brought it the second time. But usually it is harder than this. The manager might also want to know why some didn't buy or have had even heard of the product. There is rarely any time and money to study everything the manager may have to narrow things down. Developing a priority list that includes all the possible problem areas is sensible. The various items on the list may need to be considered more completely in the situation analysis step before final priorities can be set.

Step 2: Situation Analysis: When the marketing manager feels the real problem has begun to surface, a situation analysis is useful. A situation analysis is a casual study of the information that is already available in the problem area. The situation analysis may help refine the problem definition and specify what additional information if any, is needed. The situation analysis usually involves casual talks with well-informed people that is, others in the firm, a few good gentlemen who have close contact with customers, or others knowledgeable about in the industry. In industrial marketing, where relationships with customers are close the customers themselves may be called. Perhaps one of these people may have already worked on the same problem, or knows about a useful source of relevant information. Their inputs may help to sharpen the problem definition, too. The situation analysis is especially important if the researcher is a research specialist who doesn't know much about the management decisions to be made of if the marketing manager is dealing with unfamiliar areas. They must be sure that they comprehend the problem area, together with the nature of the target market, the marketing mix, competition, and external factors. Or else, the researcher may rush ahead and could end up making foolish mistakes or simply "discover" what is already known by management.

Step 3: Getting Problem-Specific Data: This stage of research calls for determining the type of information needed and the most efficient ways to gather this information. A researcher can gather secondary data, primary data or a mix of both. Secondary data is the information that is already in existence somewhere, having been collected for another purpose. The primary data consists of originally collected information for the specific purpose at hand. Primary research involves the collection of primary data by the marketing researcher or agents of the marketing researcher directly from respondents. Because these data may be collected firsthand, the process tends to be more costly and may be more time consuming than is the collection of secondary research data. However, the use of primary data is sometimes mandatory when secondary data are unavailable; the primary data are usually much more relevant to what is being researched because of the unique situation or problem, or the timing. Secondary research depends on secondary data or data obtained from sources other than directly from respondents. In other words, the research has already been accomplished. Most researchers usually begin by examining published secondary research sources to see what data already exist that have been collected for some other problem or some other purpose. In some cases, the problem has already been researched in its entirety, and the data are timely and directly relevant and applicable to the problem at hand. In such a case, use of secondary research data could save the time and money of putting together and conducting a primary research project.

Step 4: Interpretation of Data: The interpretation of marketing information is a significant nature of marketing research. The marketing information is properly interpreted and analysed. The information collected will have to be edited, coded, tabulated and analysed to interpret the facts and figures of the markets. One can see that getting a representative sample is very important. The most common method for getting a representative sample is random sampling, where each member of the population has an equal chance of being included in the sample. Great care must be used to ensure that sampling is really random and not just haphazard. The nature of the sample, and how it is selected, makes a big difference in how the results of a study can be interpreted. This should be considered as a part of planning data collection, to make sure that the final results can be interpreted with enough confidence so the marketing manager can use them in his planning. Even though the sampling may be carefully planned, it is important to evaluate the quality of the research data itself. Besides sampling and validity problems, a marketing manager should consider whether the analysis of the data supports the conclusions drawn in the interpretation step. Sometimes the technical people pick the right statistical procedure and their calculations are exact but they offer a wrong interpretation because they don't understand the management problem.

Step 5: Problem Solution: In the problem solution step, the results of the research are used in making media decisions. At the conclusion of the research process the marketing media manager should be able to apply the research findings to marketing strategy planning.

3.4 Media Selection

3.4.1 Introduction

Just like an electrical current flows from one point to the other through a conductor, likewise the advertising message is transmitted via the advertising media from the advertiser to the target market. Thus Advertising media are the vehicles which carry the advertising message. The advertiser has different kinds of media that are available at his disposal. Which one of these should be selected for a particular type of advertisement is the subject matter of this chapter. Effective advertising denotes informing the target market about the product at the right time through the right medium at an affordable cost to the company. Conveying a right message through an appropriate medium at the wrong time would surmount to wastage of valuable resources. Therefore, selecting the right media is the core of success of the entire advertising campaign. However, an appropriate timing and the right place of advertising is of equal importance.

The decisions of media selection refers only to the selection of a single specific medium of advertising, such as the newspaper, magazine, radio, television, mail service or outdoor advertising. In contrast to media planning which is a general term encompassing a variety of decisions involved at the time and place of advertising in bundled with the selection of the medium. A media plan lays out advertising time and space in various media that will be used to achieve the marketing objectives of the organisation through effective advertising. The significance of advertising and its role as a powerful marketing tool has been dealt with earlier.

Promotion is one of the 4 Ps forming the marketing mix, and advertising is an important part of it. An advertising plan is based on an overall promotional strategy; and media planning follows the advertising plan. Media strategy is thus a part of the marketing strategy.

In other words, the media plan is part of the overall market plan, and media selection is the last stage in the process of promotion through advertising. Media decisions are mainly concerned with the following:

What are the available media which will serve our advertising needs best?

Examples: Newspaper, magazine, radio, television, direct mailing, outdoor, etc.

Which individual medium in each general category of media selected above will be the best vehicle for our advertising?

Examples: TOI, India Today, Mumbai-Pune-Nagpur radio and Mumbai TV commercials. What could be the best combination or mix of media for our total advertising? What would be the best specific schedule for the release of our ads in each of these media?

Media planning and media selection assume significance in the light of frequent reports that advertising is wasteful. One advertiser confessed: "Half of the advertising efforts are wasted. But the issue is I don't know which half is being wasted." By following the correct methodology and using quantitative models in media planning, elimination of wasteful advertising can be achieved to a great extent. This is true because, in the entire advertising cost, the substantial amount of advertising is paid as media charges. The effectiveness of a well-designed advertising message majorly depends upon "when" and "where" it is released. These are "time" and "place" decisions. In short, it may be said that the success of advertising majorly depends upon the selection of right media and timely release of the advertisement message. The frequency, continuity and the place of its release also has importance in the success of the advertising campaign.

3.4.2 Approaches

Strategy is one of the more important words in a media selection professional's vocabulary. The times when print, television, and radio were the only avenues to get a client's message out are long gone. Though they are still important and hold a significant place it is important that a media selection professional also considers the rapid evolution of "new" media.

Identifying the appropriate channels for the clients is a very difficult task. Should you use facebook or should you stick to regular emailing? Should you use YouTube to get a product get more visibility or would blogging be better option? Using a well-developed strategy can be of a great help in selecting media. Without a proper strategy, plans are nothing more than words on paper; having said that, it's important to make the strategic approach a solid one.

1. **The SWOT analysis:** This is a key tool in strategic planning. It helps to determine the direction of the campaign. By delving into the SWOT, we understand the media outlets that we must focus on.

2. **Relationship building:** There is a huge number of advantages of relationships that we establish. When the media selector is attempting to determine which path to use, the relationships he has built will be very handy.

3. **Social networking:** Each social media channel has a different audience, and hence they need to be treated as such. Facebook, Twitter, YouTube Etc. has different audience hence the approach of each product on each of these medias must be unique in its own way.

3.4.3 Factors Affecting Selection of Media

1. **The nature of the product:** The nature of the product determines the media to be used. If the product is such that it is used by one and all then a mass media like print, broadcast and outdoor will be used. However, if the product is such that it is used only by a select audience, for example say doctors, then magazine media and direct mail may be used. If the product is such that it requires demonstration then television will be the main media. However, fairs and exhibitions may also be used and newspapers can also act as supplementary media for this product. Thus, the advertiser chooses that media which matches his product and its nature.

2. **Potential market:** The choice of media also depends upon the characteristics of the target audience. If the message is to reach people with a higher income, magazine is the best medium. If a local area is to be covered, newspapers and outdoor advertising media are of much help. However, if the audience comprises of illiterate folks too, then they can be reached through radio, film and television advertising.

3. **The type of distribution strategy:** There is a direct co-relationship between the advertising and distribution strategy of the company. Thus, a company should select that media for advertising its products which matches its distribution strategy. Thus, there is no point in advertising a product if it is not available in those outlets where the target consumer normally buys his products. Similarly, the advertiser need not advertise on the national media if he does not have a national distribution system.

4. **The advertising objective:** The advertising objective that the advertiser wants to achieve through the advertising campaign, also affects the choice of media. Though the major objective of every advertising campaign is to influence the consumer positively towards the advertised product and the company; the specific objectives maybe to have a local, regional or national coverage; to have immediate or delayed action; to create primary or secondary demand. If he wants to achieve immediate action in reply to his advertising message, direct advertising is the answer. If he wants to build up goodwill for the company, newspaper and magazine are a better choice of media. If he wants a national coverage he can go for newspaper, magazines, radio, television and film advertising.

5. **The type of selling message:** The selection of media also depends upon the type of advertising message which is to be conveyed. If the message is such that it will require colour in order to appeal then magazine, film and television advertising media will be most suitable. If the message is such that a demonstration is necessary

then television and film media would be ideal. If timeliness is of prime importance then media such as newspapers, radio and posters can be used. Thus, the type of advertising message influences the choice of media.

6. **Budget:** The amount of budget available will also decide the media used. If the budgeted funds are large, there is no limit to the choice of media. However, if the budget is small then it automatically rules out the expensive media.

7. **Competitive advertising:** While selecting the media the advertiser must keep an eye on the media selected by his competitors. Some media are known as prestige media. Advertising through these media (like television) gives a prestigious effect to the product advertised. Thus, if the competitor is using a prestige media and our company is not doing so, we may lose out in the market. Thus, in order to stay on par with the competition it is necessary to keep in mind the competitor's choice of media while making our own media decisions. Not only should an eye be kept on the competitor's choice of media, but also on the industry trends in general. This is because you can benefit from the past experience of the industry in choice of media. However, it is not necessary that you should always follow the beaten track. Sometimes, new decisions regarding media may prove to be a successful change.

8. **Media availability:** Another aspect of choice of media is its availability. The required media time and space should be available. Sometimes, it so happens that, the desired time and space in media is not available. In such a situation the advertiser has no choice but to make a compromise and use the available media time and space.

9. **Characteristics of media:** Media characteristics differ from media to media and these characteristics have a bearing on their choice. These media characteristics are as follows.

   • **Coverage:** Media coverage refers to the circulation of the media. Advertisers normally prefer media with a larger coverage or circulation. The larger the coverage the greater the chances of message exposure to the audience. Media such as newspapers, magazines, radio and television are known for their mass coverage. On the other hand direct advertising, outdoor advertising media are known for local and regional coverage.

   • **Reach:** As compared to coverage, reach is a better measure for finding out the effectiveness of an advertising message. Reach is the medium's access to different individuals or homes over a given period of time. Thus, we talk of readership in case of press media, listenership in case of radio, and viewership in case of television. In fact, reach studies are of vital significance in evaluating the strength of a media means. The advertiser is more interested in the actual number of persons or the homes covered than how many are subscribing to the newspapers and magazines or how many have radios or television sets. In fact, it is the actual and the potential reach of a medium that is more important.

- **Relative cost:** Relative cost refers to the amount of money spent on using a particular medium. In the case of magazines it is the rate per page per thousand users. In the case of radio and television it is per thousand listeners or viewers. Relative cost calculations take into account both circulation and the impact the medium has on the audience. He selects that medium with the least cost to get the best results for a rupee spent by him.

- **Consumer confidence:** Consumer confidence is another factor to be taken into account while evaluating the advertising medium. Consumer confidence or credibility refers to the confidence placed in the medium by the consumers. This consumer credibility of a medium is important because, the credibility of the advertising message depends upon it.

- **Frequency:** Frequency refers to the number of times an audience is reached in a given period of time. Newspapers, television, radio and outdoor media are known for highest degree of frequency. Magazines, display and direct advertising have a lower frequency. Closely related to frequency is the point of continuity. Continuity refers to the time sequence of advertisements especially the time that elapses between the deliveries of successive messages to the audiences. This is of top significance to fight the problems of forgetting and competition.

However, while deciding on the choice of media all the above points should be considered and that media should be chosen which suits the needs of the advertiser as well as gives him the maximum for every rupee spent on advertising.

Designing media plan – The target market – The type of the product to be advertised – Characteristics of distribution channel – Copy formulation – Exposure to the product.

Points to Remember

- In advertising terms **Medium** is a channel of communication such as newspapers, magazines, radio and television. It is also a vehicle for carrying the sales message of an advertiser to the prospects and it is also a vehicle by which advertisers convey their messages to a large group of prospects and thereby aid in closing the gap between the producer at one end and the consumer on the other.

- **Advertising Media** are the physical means whereby a manufacturer of goods or utilities or a supplier of services tells the consumer about his product or service.

- **Indoor Advertising** means those media that reach the audience right inside their houses or indoors. These vehicles are newspapers, radios, televisions and films.

- **Radio advertising** can aptly be called as "word of mouth" advertising. It is a medium of mass communication that appeals to the ears through sound.

- **Film advertising** is a medium of publicity characterised by sound, motion, colour, vision and timeliness. It is like a television run on an enlarged screen for a larger audience.

- **Web Banner Advertising** is a type of Internet advertising whereby one pays another website the amount to display an advertising banner on their website for a certain length of time.

- **Outdoor advertising** is the oldest form of advertising. It is also known as 'position', 'mural' or 'indirect' advertising, this advertising is conducted out of the home or place of business.

- **Direct advertising** is a very comprehensive phrase covering all forms of printed advertising delivered directly to the prospective customer.

- A **Circular** is a sheet of paper or sheets of papers printed on either one or both sides, it gives information about the product in colour or in black and white.

- **Display advertising media** is also known as POP, that is, point-of-purchase advertising. It is more a promotional medium than advertising.

- A **Media Plan** outlines how advertising time and space in various media will be used to achieve the marketing objectives of the company through advertising.

- **Reach** is defined as the size of the audience who listens to, reads, views or otherwise accesses a particular advertisement in a given time period.

- **Frequency** simply measures the number of times a person sees your message in a given advertising schedule.

- **Continuity** is the Length of time that a media schedule will run it also takes into account whether it will be continuous or periodic.

Questions for Discussion

1. Explain in detail the different functions of advertising media.
2. Elaborate the difficulties faced in media planning.
3. What is the meaning of frequency and continuity in media planning? Explain.
4. Describe the different processes in media research in detail.
5. Analyse the various factors that affect selection of media.

■■■

Chapter 4...

Sales Promotion and Brand Equity

Contents ...

Learning Objectives ...

- To discuss the meaning, objectives, elements, features and types of advertising copy
- To learn about meaning and factors affecting Sales Promotion
- To understand the objectives of Sales Promotion
- To elaborate the techniques of Sales Promotion
- To study meaning and benefits of Branding
- To explain the types of brands
- To discuss the measurement and management of Branding Equity

4.1 Sales Promotion

4.1.1 Meaning and Definition

The Committee on Definition of **The American Marketing Association** defines Sales Promotion as, "*In a specific sense, Sales Promotion includes those sales activities that supplement both personal Selling and Advertising and co-ordinates them and helps to make them effective, such as, displays, shows and expositions, demonstrations and other non-recurrent selling efforts not in the ordinary routine*".

According to **A.H.R. Delens**, "Sales promotion means the steps that are taken for the purpose of obtaining an increasing sale". Often this term refers specially to selling efforts that are designed to supplement personal selling and advertising and by co-ordination helps them to become more effective."

In the words of **Roger A. Strong**, "Sales promotion includes all forms of sponsored communication apart from activities associated with personal selling. It, thus includes trade shows and exhibits, combining, sampling, premiums, trade, allowances, sales and dealer incentives, set of packs, consumer education and demonstration activities, rebates, bonus, packs, point of purchase material and direct mail."

"Sales Promotion is by and large understood and practiced as a supporting facility to Advertising and Personal Selling. It is a short term measure and is used to give the occasional boost to current sales. It does this by showing a change (though temporary) in the price value relationship of the product to the consumer. The consumer, who had so far assigned a certain value to the product, now finds an extra value in the product. Sales Promotion achieves this by lowering the price of the product or increasing its value or by resorting to both these routes."

A marketing organisation uses sales promotion techniques to persuade and influence both the dealers and the consumers. Each of these techniques communicates with the dealers and the consumers in a different way. Thus, sales promotion techniques are basically of two types. Techniques used to aid dealers and techniques used to influence consumers.

4.1.2 Objectives of Sales Promotion

The basic objective of all sales promotion activity is to increase the sale of the product or service. However, increase in sale is achieved in the below mentioned ways, which are the supplementary objectives of sale promotion activities.

1. **To introduce new products or services:** Sales promotion activities are an interesting way of introducing new products and services. Usually, free samples are provided either directly to consumers or in a "free on the purchase of a particular related item" scheme.

2. **To attract new customers:** Another objective of sales promotion schemes is to attract new customers thereby increasing the customer base of the product/service. Samples, gifts, prizes, etc. are used to increase the customer base.

3. **To induce existing customers to buy more:** Sales promotion devices are most often used to induce the existing customers of a firm to buy more. Product development, offering three products at the cost of two, discount coupons, are some of the sales promotion devices used by firms to motivate the existing buyers to buy more of a specific product.

4. **To Keep existing Customers:** A firm usually engages in a sales promotion activity to keep its existing customers, especially in a situation where a new competitive product has just been introduced and the marketer feels the treat of a movement of his customers towards the competitors product.

5. **Helps the firm to face competitive:** The industrial area today is most competitive. No company can survive without doing its utmost to attract the consumer. Thus sales promotion activities are undertaken in order to face the competitive market scenario.

6. **To increase sales in off-seasons:** Many products are seasonal and required only during particular seasons. Sales promotion activities for such products are undertaken in the off season to encourage sales of such products in seasons when they are not required.

7. **To ease the work of dealers:** The selling activity of dealers like wholesalers and retailers becomes easier when the manufacturer supplements their efforts by sales promotion measures.

8. **Inventory Clearance:** Sales promotion activities are organised with the objective of clearing the old stock to make way for new stock.

9. **Reaching New Market:** To reach a new target segment could be another objective of a sales promotion activity. For example a health club may want to attract senior citizens and as such come up with a discounted rate plan for senior citizens only.

10. **Increased Brand Awareness:** A sales promotion can help increase awareness of your brand, which can ultimately lead to additional sales.

4.1.3 Factors Affecting Sales Promotion Growth

1. **Increasing Competition:** The increasing competition is one of the factors responsible for the growth in sales promotion techniques. These techniques provide a competitive edge to the marketers.

2. **Customers Have Become More Price Sensitive:** With the increase in the number of similar products in the market the consumer has become very price sensitive. This is another reason for the growth of sales promotions.

3. **Sales Promotions Generally Create:** An immediate positive impact on sales: This is one of the major reasons for the growth and proliferation of sales promotion activities. These messages create urgency in the consumer to buy by stating that the benefits of the sales promotion are available only now.

4. **Products have become more standardised:** The current business climate is such that there are a lot of similar products in the market. Thus the consumer has a choice to buy from many available similar products. In such a business scenario, a sales promotion tends to tilt the customer in favour of the product being promoted. This has led to an increase in sales promotions.

5. **Consumer Acceptance**: As competition intensifies and promotions proliferate, consumers have learnt to earn the rewards of being smart shoppers. Over a period of time, they have also learnt that brands on promotion are not necessarily of lower quality. In fact the consumers even time their purchases in such a way that they take advantage of the various sales promotion activities.

6. **Advertising Has Become More Expensive And Less Effective:** Advertising is quite expensive. One of the major costs of advertising is the cost of media. Audio-visual medium, which is considered as the most effective for short-duration ads, may cost in excess of ` 1 lakh for a 10 second exposure during prime time. Further, consumers have reached a point of boredom due to excessive advertising on TV. Some consumers even consider advertising as an intrusion into their privacy, leading to channel switching during commercial breaks. Firms with small budgets cannot compete with big companies, which spend huge sums of money on advertising. For these small budget firms, sales promotion is a more cost-effective promotion method to produce sales results.

7. **Channel Members Have Become More Powerful:** Retailers and wholesalers have become powerful and find themselves in a position to demand extra facilities from the companies. The channel members demand more incentives to get the desired results. The manufacturers do not seem to have any alternatives but to concede to their demands, keeping in view the competitive market conditions. In shopping malls like Globus and Lifestyle, decent margins have to be paid to them in order to have shelf visibility for the brand.

8. **Increase in Profits:** Sales promotion activities help an organisation to maximise profits. Promotions that offer discounted prices enable a premium brand to compete with a lower tier brand among price sensitive consumers. Thereby, increasing the market share and profits for the brand.

9. **Introducing an Element of Interest:** There are a number of promotions, which are often called interest promotions. Some of the more popular interest promotion techniques are samples, contests, and sweepstakes, free premiums and mail-in premiums. These promotions create an element of interest and excitement, and consumers enjoy these and respond enthusiastically to such contests and sweepstakes. An ideal example is the sweepstakes organized by readers digest every year.

10. **Increase in Impulse buying:** The increase in the number of huge malls with a large number of shops and huge displays has led to an increase in impulse buying. Sales promotions further give an impetus to impulse buying.

11. **Excess Stocks:** Due to the increase in the number of similar products and brands, it is difficult for the manufacturers to perfectly estimate the demand. When huge excess stocks are left with the manufacturers they have no choice but to dispense with them through sales promotion activities.

4.1.4 Techniques of Sales Promotion

(A) Sales Promotion Techniques used to aid dealers:

It is through the dealers that the manufacturer sells his products. If the dealer is efficient and sells a vast amount of the manufacturer's products, the manufacturer tends to gain. Thus, many manufacturers help their dealers and middlemen to increase the sales of their products in many ways. Some of these are as under:

1. **Provision of Management Aid:** Manufacturers provide technical guidance to the dealers. This guidance takes many forms, like, assistance in scientific layout of stores, arrangement of goods in the stores, good lighting and ventilation arrangement etc.

2. **Communicating Marketing Information:** The manufacturer communicates information about his products, as well as competing products, so that the dealers are well informed and can better sell the products.

3. **Training of Dealers:** The manufacturers organise training programmes for the dealers, whereby the dealers polish up their sales and marketing skills.

4. **Furnish the Dealer with Sales literature and Display material:** The dealers are supplied with all kinds of sales literature like pamphlets, circulars and booklets that aid him in making sales. Sometimes dealers are supplied with display material which attracts the attention of the consumer to the product. For example, beautiful net baskets that display Maggie Noodles or Fritto Lays.

5. **Attractive Terms of Sale:** The dealers are offered attractive terms of sale, credit facility and take back offers in order to aid them in increasing the sales of the product.

6. **Dealer Contests:** Many a times manufacturers organise contests between dealers and give awards and prizes to the dealers who has the highest turnover or the best window display for a particular product. Sometimes, awards are also given for the amount of visibility maintained by dealers for the manufacturers' product etc.

(B) Sales Promotion Techniques that Influence the Consumer

1. **Sales Promotion Letters:** Several large companies use the medium of letters for sales promotion. These letters serve different purposes. Sometimes, they are used to give information about the company's products; while, all other times, they are reminders to buy a particular brand. Some letters seek information from customers on various aspects of their purchases. Studies conducted on the efficacy of letters as a medium of sales promotion indicate that a good letter must seek action from the receiver. Sales promotion letters are sent to salesmen, dealers and consumers.

2. **Catalogues:** Catalogues carry essential information on the products offered by the company. Well-designed catalogues give complete information relating to products, their pictures, size specifications, colours, packing, uses and prices. The products are properly listed and indexed to facilitate order booking and processing. Everything about the catalogue, right from the quality of paper used to the colours, pictures and information communicates with the audience.

3. **POP/Display:** Point of Purchase Promotion (POP) is one of the most widely used sales promotional tools. It is also sometimes referred to as point of sales promotion. With the proliferation of brands, innovative displays have become a prerequisite for success. Brands compete with each other for consumer's attention and for shelf space. The need to remain on top of the consumer's mind has become the prime concern of marketers. Hence, the importance of POP displays.

   Various kinds of display materials like posters, danglers, stickers, mobile wobblers and streamers are used at the retail shop level to induce purchase. In the modem context of high intensity marketing, the retailers are virtually flooded with POPs by all manufacturers. If they are just dumped in a forsaken corner of the shop, the brand does not get the intended sales promotional benefit from the POPs. Only those who can manage to get the right display effect will benefit from POPs.

   To enhance the display effect, manufacturers use several gadgets and approaches. Illuminated designs, motion displays, etc., add to the display effect. Some companies organise display units and locate them at vantage points within the store attracting the attention of store traffic. Skillfully designed and strategically located display units can enhance the sales appeal. More and more firms are going in for innovative displays to give their brands visibility in today's crowded shop shelves. When Nestle' launched Maggi Noodles, way back in 1983, they used a unique dispenser, the wire mesh bag. Not only did it help in brand identification, it was helpful to the retailer too. The dispenser hung from the ceiling helped him to save shelf space. Cadbury too came out with a dispenser. Companies are also using the technique of mass display. Within the limited space available in the retail store, big stocks of a given brand are artistically arranged to gain attention. Customised racks are also being used for display effect. In fact, in many companies today, salesmen are evaluated not only on achievement of sales quota but also on factors like, the number of displays organised for the company.

Displays have their origins in the age-old belief that goods well displayed are half sold. Displays can be of various types (1) window displays, (2) wall displays, (3) counter displays or (4) floor displays.

4. **Demonstrations:** Companies resort to product demonstrations for sales promotion, especially, when they are coming up with a new product. In India, in recent years, several products - low unit price products like beverages and washing powders as well as high unit price products like washing machines and personal computers - have utilised product demonstration as a tool of sales promotion.

5. **Demonstrations at Retail Stores and Malls:** Sometimes, demonstrations are organised at retail stores by company salesmen for the benefit of retailers as well as consumers. Many cosmetic companies organise free make-up demonstrations at their counters in huge malls.

6. **Door to Door Demonstrations:** Consumer product companies quite often resort to house-to-house (door-to-door) demonstrations. It is considered a highly specialised field of sales promotion. Salesmen employed for such demonstrations are given special training to handle peculiar situations involved in this field.

7. **Demonstrations to Key People:** Sometimes, demonstrations are organised for the benefit of key people and influential persons. Journalists, and other media men, community leaders, etc., are invited and the product is introduced to them. Demonstration is a good selling technique which involves the co-operation of sales representatives and prospective consumers in the actual process of demonstration of the product. Participation of the consumer persuades him to learn more about the product and it serves as a persuasion for him to try the product. Many software companies also organise seminars and workshops for key and influential people. In the course of the workshop, a demonstration of the product takes place. Thus, the marketer brings the right people in the right environment, gets their exclusive attention and then makes a demonstration and influences the audience in favour of his product.

8. **Trade Fairs and Exhibitions:** Trade fairs and exhibitions are extensively used as sales promotion tools. They also form one of the oldest practices in sales promotion. Trade fairs and exhibitions provide companies with the opportunity of introducing and displaying their products. This brings the company's products and consumers in direct contact with each other. 'Seeing is believing' is a concept behind large scale exhibitions. In the case of high cost industrial products, a trade fair is the most handy and effective sales promotion tool. Especially, in international marketing, international trade fairs are the methods commonly resorted to. Orders and inquiries worth billions get generated at international trade fairs. Coupons, premiums, free offers, price-offs, extras, instalment, payment offers coupons, premiums, free offers, price-offs, etc., have become common and effective sales promotion tools.

9. **Coupons:** Coupons are certificates which offer price reductions to consumers for specified items. They are distributed through newspaper and magazine advertisements or, with the package of the merchandise or, even by direct mail. Coupons normally perform two specific functions for the manufacturer. Firstly, they enthuse the consumers to exploit the bargain. Secondly, they serve as an inducement to the channel for stocking the items. The manufacturer, thus, succeeds in attracting consumers as well as in prompting the channel to stock the merchandise through introducing coupons. They are useful for introducing a new product as well as for strengthening the sale of an existing product.

10. **Premiums and Free Offers:** In the Indian markets today, premiums, free offers and price-offs are extensively used by manufacturers and marketers. 'Buy one get one free', 'buy two get two free', 'buy two get three free', 'book a house get a car free', 'book a house get the interior done for free' are some of the offers doing the rounds today. All these communicate more value for the product, and do influence the audience decision-making process.

11. **Price-off:** Hawkins pressure cookers have come up with several sales promotion schemes during the last few years. In one of these schemes - Hawkins announced: 'Up to ₹ 150 off on a new Hawkins in exchange for any old pressure cooker'. And, the ad specified that the offer is open only up to a particular date.

12. **Free Samples of the Product:** Free samples are offered to persuade consumers to try them out. By offering free samples to a large section of a new market, a company tries to gain entry into that market. Of course, the constraint in utilising this tool is that the product should be of low unit cost and susceptible to frequent repeat purchases. Soaps, detergents, coffee and toothpastes are examples of products which are normally popularised by providing free samples. In fact, even newspapers, are being introduced and popularised through this method.

13. **Gifts:** Companies also distribute gifts to people - customers, dealers, and influential and key people. These gifts include pens, pencils, calendars, diaries, table decorations, etc. Gifts carry the company's name and logo. The gifts are intended to create goodwill towards the company and indirectly promote the company's sales interest.

14. **Contests:** Contests of various kinds constitute another widely and commonly used sales promotion tool. There are 'dealer contests' meant exclusively for dealers of the company and 'consumer contests' open for all. Companies use both dealer contests and consumer contests. While dealer contests normally remain a closed affair between the company and its dealers, consumer contests are given wide publicity to attract the participation of a widely scattered consumer base. Big outlays are naturally allocated for consumer contests because they need wide publicity and attractive prizes.

15. **Consumer Contests:** Consumer contests take a variety of forms - quiz contests, beauty contests, scooter and car rallies, lucky draws, suggesting a brand name, coining a slogan, suggesting a logo, etc. whatever be the type of contest - filling up the quiz, writing 25 words about the brand, or taking part in a rally - the intention of the marketer is to create widespread action and news around the brand. To get the consumer interested in the brand and induce him to buy it is the central idea in all consumer contests.

16. **Sponsoring Major National International Events:** When major national and international events take place, the companies concerned associate themselves with such events, spending a lot of money. The field of sports usually provides maximum number of such events. Business firms either sponsor the event as a whole, or take the lead role in specific aspects associated with the event. Watch manufacturers take up the role of official time keepers in such events, and soft drinks and food chains take up the role of official suppliers of soft drinks and food items. The intention is to remain part of the news creating event and reap the best of sales promotional benefits from associations. Such efforts also form part of sales promotion. Today, companies like, Kingfisher Airlines, Idea Cellular, Coca Cola, DLF and Hero Honda among many others are sponsoring the DLF IPL cricket matches.

Apart from winning the right to sponsor an event which is just the beginning of the sales promotional effort, the companies concerned have to effectively promote the event and construct a whole set of marketing activities around the event. How companies use promotions to get more reward out of sponsorships is the real test. So, while sponsoring sports events, the sponsor is likely to run promotional contests for dealers and consumers for generating excitement through dealer promotion, and consumer participation.

17. **Sales Promotion through Merchandising:** Though merchandising is not an integral part of sales promotion, in view of the close linkage between the two, a reference to merchandising would be essential in the discussion on sales promotion. Good merchandising at the store level often prompts the buyer in different ways: to buy 'now' rather than later, buy more than the originally intended quantity or buy a particular pack size in preference to another. All these are essentially sales promotional objectives. While advertising can only make a consumer aware of the product or generate in him a desire for it, merchandising, in many cases, instantly motivates a consumer to buy a product.

Merchandising activity can be rightly described as a 'clincher' in the marketing process. After all, the word 'merchandise' means 'goods for sale', and the term 'merchandising' embraces all activities undertaken at the retail shop to promote sales. In particular, it includes two elements - imaginative use of dealer service material, and alluring display of products in the retail outlet. As such, it is but apt that merchandising is well recognised for its sales promotional role. In some cases, merchandising is particularly effective in inducing-brand switching.

A consumer normally goes to a retail outlet to purchase his usual brand. At the retail outlet, a good display of a competing brand can command his attention and he may ultimately buy the competing brand. In other words, merchandising can lead to impulse buying and through that process to brand switching.

4.2 Strategic Sales Promotion

4.2.1 Strategies and Practices in Sales Promotion

Some of the strategies and practices in sales promotion like cross promotion, surrogate selling, bait and switch advertising issues are dealt with here.

4.2.2 Cross Promotion

Cross promotion is a form of advertising that involves two or more parties. It is a way in which two parties help each other to promote each other's product. What happens is each party helps to promote the other party's product or service. A good example of an effective cross promotion campaign is the Visa Card. Visa tends to use this technique a lot. What they do is mention a store or whatever in their commercials. Let's say it's a dot com. Yourname.com will make a good example. Their commercials will talk about all that you can buy on "Yourname.com," and what a great place it is for buying that product. Then their ads will mention the visa credit card is some way, shape, or form. In turn, "Yourname.com" will recommend that their customers use their visa cards to make any purchases from the website. There will probably also be ads, and maybe even credit applications.

There are several different forms of cross promotion, but this is the most common. Basically what you are doing is getting other companies to promote your product. The just completed Commonwealth Games is another example of cross promotions. Many companies helped to promote the Commonwealth Games by calling themselves Sponsors of the Commonwealth Games 2010. In return, they got to not only place ads and banners around the various events, but use the brand name of the Commonwealth Games to add credibility to their product.

Cross promotion is used by organisations to stand out from their competition in a crowded advertising marketplace. They are used by businesses, non-profit government agencies to "outmarket" bigger competitors. Cross-promotions include "bundled" offerings, joint media appearances and events, and unconventional cause-related marketing. It might also include collaboratively produced how-to's and other resource booklets and videos, co-branding, co-op advertising, and shared space.

Cross-promotion has the potential for a big marketing payoff because partners can successfully expand through each other's customer base. They can gain an inexpensive and credible introduction to more of their kind of customer more effectively than with the traditional "solo" methods of networking, advertising, or public relations.

Given below are some creative ways of cross-promotion:

- Printed joint promotional messages on receipts.
- Offering a reduced price, special service, or convenience if customers buy products from both the partners.
- Hanging signs or posters promoting one another on your walls, windows, or products.
- Mentioning one another's benefits when you speak at local events or are interviewed by the media.
- Dropping one another's flyers in shopping bags.
- Pool mailing lists and send out a joint promotional postcard.
- Giving a joint interview to a local media.
- Giving your partner's product to your customers when they buy a large quantity of your product, and ask your partner to do the same.
- Using door hangers, posters, flyers, or postcards to promote special offers for each other's products.

4.2.3 Surrogate Selling

Ever wondered why Bacardi and Kingfisher manufacturers and marketers of liquor started manufacturing and marketing mineral water?

The answer to this is surrogate advertising.

The makers of these brands were banned to advertise their products on national television and hence they resorted to surrogate advertising. Surrogate advertising is a sort of advertising where a cover product is promoted in order to promote the actual product that is banned.

A surrogate advertising campaign can be used to indirectly promote products or services deemed by some groups as being unhealthy, unethical, and immoral or, possibly, illegal through activities that are viewed as acceptable forms of promotion. For instance, in some parts of the world where regulation exists that may ban promoting alcohol and tobacco, firms promote these brands by tying the brand names to more acceptable products. For instance, the same brand name used for selling cigarettes may also be the same brand name on health product. In this way the customer is not only aware of the acceptably advertised brand but also understands the connection to the regulated product.

In India, ministry of health has banned the advertising of liquor and tobacco. But many liquor brands (like McDowell's whisky) initiated other products like sodas in the same name which are then advertised. Another instance of surrogate advertising is 'Four Square Bravery Awards' in the name of Four Square cigarettes.

4.2.4 Bait and Switch Advertising Issues

Illegal practice that employs 'bait and switch pricing,' is also called as bait advertising.

Bait and switch advertising is a common form of false advertising. It occurs when a seller advertises a bargain on an item to attract a customer to the store. When the customer arrives at the store he finds that the item is 'sold out'. The seller then offers the customer another item which is usually more expensive.

The purpose of the bait and switch tactic is to get customers to visit a store or business by advertising very low prices. Once the customer is in the store, the salespeople attempt to offer the customer items at higher prices.

The bait and switch begins with the bait, an advertisement for a product at what seems like an extremely low price. Sometimes these products, such as mattresses, are of very low quality. At other times, the price may apply to one specific style of, or model of an item. In general, the bait is stocked in very low numbers. In some cases, only one or two of items are available at the low price.

Once the customer has walked into the retail establishment the bait and switch moves to the switch. The salesperson will inform the customer that the store has sold out of the advertised item and offers a similar item at a higher price. Alternately the salesperson may push hard to be certain the customer understands that the lower-priced product is of inferior quality, and try to sell a better quality product at a higher price. Bait and switch may also be used to bring in customers with bait, low prices, and also raise prices of unrelated items that customers might also pick up at the time.

To avoid prosecution for bait and switch tactics, advertisements frequently place in small print that, the item is limited to the quantity in the store. Reading the fine print of an advertisement can often alert customers that the advertisement is clearly employing bait and switch tactics.

4.3 Branding

4.3.1 Introduction

Let us begin with the traditional meaning of the word "Brand". The term brand was originally associated with 'an identifying mark burned on livestock or (especially in former times) criminals or slaves with a branding iron'. Today, thanks to modern technology and a courageous battle for civil rights, both of the above mentioned practices cease to exist.

So what is a brand in the 21st century? Let us start with a few examples of some brand names. Google, Apple, Xerox, Kellogg's, Maggie, Walkman. The mere mention of these names draws an immediate mental picture of the products endorsed by them. These brands have succeeded in making an impression on the minds of billions of people. If you haven't heard of these names, then that's probably because the medium used by the brand isn't one that you are a part of. For example, if a brand has taken to the Internet to advertise its existence and the products it has in its portfolio and you are one who isn't active on the Internet, then the brand hasn't reached out to you. Such cases of using only a select media for propagating brands are best avoided while building a successful brand that would stand the test of time.

Keeping with this forward-looking approach to branding let's try and establish a current and updated definition of a brand. To understand what the term 'brand' means today one has to study every aspect of its evolution.

A brand is an identifying symbol, words or mark that distinguishes a product or company from its competitors. According to the **American Marketing Association Dictionary,** *"A brand is a name, term, design, or other feature that distinguishes one seller's product from those of others".* A modern example of a brand is MacBook that belongs to a company called Apple Inc.

According to **Philip Kotler**, "A brand is a name, term, sign, symbol, or design or a combination of these, intended to identify the goods or services of one seller or a group of sellers and to differentiate them from those of the competitors.

Brands are generally developed over time through:

1. Advertisements containing consistent messaging.
2. Recommendations from friends, family members or colleagues.
3. Interactions with a company and its representatives.

4. Real-life experiences using a product or service (generally considered the most important element of a brand).

5. Once developed, brands generally provide an umbrella under which many different products can be offered providing a company tremendous economic leverage and strategic advantage in generating awareness of their offerings in the market place.

4.3.2 Terminology

1. **Brand Name** is that part that can be spoken. This would include letters, words and numbers, for example 7Up. Brand names simplify shopping, guarantee a certain level of quality and allow for self-expression.

2. **Brand Mark:** Elements of the brand that cannot be spoken, for example, symbol.

3. **Trade Character:** For example, Ronald McDonald, Pillsbury Doughboy.

4. **Trademark:** Legal designation that the owner has exclusive rights to the brand or part of a brand.

5. **Trade Name:** The full legal name of the organisation, for example "Ford"; not the name of a specific product.

However a brand is more than just a name or symbol. It is a set of perceptions and images that represent a product, service or company. While many people refer to a brand as a logo, sign, design or symbol, a brand actually is much larger. A brand is the essence or promise of what will be delivered or experienced. A brand represents everything that the product or service means to the consumer.

The marketing strategy employed in creating a brand is known as "branding". Branding has become so important that today hardly any product is unbranded. All products right from shoes to salt are branded and sold. This is because branding provides many benefits to both the buyer and the seller.

4.3.3 Types of Brands

When deciding upon the sponsorship of a brand, the manufacturer has the following four options.

1. **Manufacturer's Brand:** When a manufacturer decides to market his product under his own brand name, it is known as a 'manufacturer's brand'. A manufacturer's brand is also known as a 'national brand'. Almost all manufacturers create their own brands. For example, Kellogg's, IBM, Cadbury's etc. Manufacturer's brands have dominated the retail industry from a very long period of time.

2. **Store Brand or Distributor's Brand or Private Brand:** In recent times, an increasing number of retailers and wholesalers have created their own brands or store brands. For example, all big retail malls have their own in-house brands. Private brands can be hard to establish and costly to stock and promote. However, they also yield higher

profit margins for the reseller. These brands also give the retailer exclusive products that cannot be bought from the competitors, resulting in greater store traffic and loyalty. Retailers price their store brands lower than comparable manufacturer's brands, thereby appealing to budget-conscious shoppers. As store brands improve in quality and, as consumers gain confidence in their store chains, they are posing a strong challenge to manufacturer's brands.

3. **Licensing:** Many manufacturers spend a lot of time and money in creating their own brands. However, there are some companies that licence names and symbols previously created, of well-known celebrities or characters from popular movies and books, by other manufacturers, for a fee. When one of these is licensed for a fee and used as a brand it is known as 'licensing'. These provide the licensee with an instant proven brand.

    Clothes and accessories sellers pay large royalties to adorn their products with the names or initials of well-known designers like Calvin Klein, Tommy Hilfiger, Gucci, or Armani. Sellers of children's products attach an endless list of character names to products used by children like clothing, toys, school supplies, stationery items, lunch boxes etc. Licensed character names range from power puff girls to Pokemon to Harry Potter characters. Almost half of retail toy sales come from products based on television shows and movies like He-Man, Spiderman, Batman, Lion King, Scooby Doo, Harry Potter etc. Names and character licensing has been growing phenomenally in recent years.

4. **Co-branding:** Co-branding occurs when two established brand names of different companies are used on the same product. For example, Kellogg's joined with ConAgra to co-brand healthy choice from Kellogg's Cereal. In most co-branding situations, one company licenses another company's well known brand to use in combination with its own.

    Co-branding offers many advantages. Because each brand dominates in a different category, the combined brands create broader consumer appeal and greater brand equity. Co-branding also allows a company to expand its existing brand into a category it might otherwise have difficulty entering alone. For example, by licensing its healthy choice brand to Kellogg's, ConAgra entered the breakfast segment and, in return, Kellogg's, could leverage the broad awareness of the healthy choice name in the cereal category.

4.3.4 Benefits of Branding

(A) Benefits of Brands to Sellers

1. Branding helps a seller to differentiate his products from the competitors' products.
2. Branding identifies a company's products making repeat sales easier for customers.

3. Branding facilitates promotional efforts.
4. Branding reduces price comparisons.
5. The seller's brand name and trademark provide legal protection for unique product features that otherwise might be copied by the competitors.
6. Branding helps the seller to segment the market.
7. Branding helps achieve easier co-operation with intermediaries, especially for known brands.
8. Branding helps a seller charge a premium price for the product.
9. Branding helps the seller in the introduction of new products.
10. Branding helps in creation of brand loyalty and thereby promoting a stable market for the sellers' products.

(B) Benefits of Brands to Buyers

Branding helps buyers in many ways.

1. Branding helps customers identify the products and services of a seller or a group of sellers.
2. It helps customers identify products that they like/ dislike.
3. Branding helps reduce shopping time.
4. Branding helps customers to identify the quality of the product.
5. Branding helps the customers to know about the features and benefits of the product.
6. It helps reduce the buyer's perceived risk of purchase.
7. Branding helps buyers derive a psychological reward from owning a particular brand like Rolex watch or Mercedes car.

4.4 Brand Equity

4.4.1 Concept of Brand Equity

Brand equity is the higher value that a company can get on the sale of a branded product as compared to a generic product. For example the price of a Bata sports shoe is much higher than the price of a non-branded sports shoe. Brand equity is created when the consumers perceives the product to have a high degree of quality. When a company organises its marketing communication in such a way that the brand gains recognition in the market, becomes easily recognisable and widely visible, the chances of gaining a higher price premium and thereby high brand equity becomes possible. Advertising through a mass marketing medium or undertaking a mass marketing campaign too helps in creating brand equity.

4.4.2 Brand Equity Defined

Marketers and researchers use various perspectives to study brand equity. Customer based approaches view brand equity from the perspective of the consumer. This consumer may be an individual consumer or an organisation.

- The **American Marketing Association** defines brand equity from a consumer perspective as "brand equity is based on consumer attitudes about positive brand attributes and favourable consequences of brand use."

- According to **Lance Leuthesser** (**1995**) "... brand equity represents the value (to a consumer) of a product, above that which would result for an otherwise identical product without the brand's name. In other words, brand equity represents the degree to which a brand's name alone contributes value to the offering (again, from the perspective of the consumer)."

- The **Marketing Science Institute (1988)** defines brand equity as, "The set of associations and behaviours on the part of the brand's customers, channel members, and parent corporations that permit the brand to earn greater volume or greater margins than it could without the brand name and that gives the brand a strong, sustainable, and differentiated advantage over competitors."

4.4.3 Brand Criteria / Brand Elements Choice Criteria

Brand Elements: Brand elements are those trademarkable devices that serve to identify and differentiate the brand. Most brands employ multiple brand elements. These elements include the logo, slogan, mascot, jingles, packages, signages as well as the brand name.

Brand element Choice Criteria: A brand element is used because the marketer expects it to fulfill the following criteria

1. Memorable 2. Meaningful 3. Likeable 4. Protectable 5. Adaptable and 6. Transferable

The first three criteria that is "memorable, meaningful and likeable" can be characterised as brand building criteria as if these criteria are there in the elements chosen to help in the brand building process.

The next three criteria that is "Protectable, adaptable and transferable' can be characterised as brand preserving criteria as these are concerned with maintaining the brand in the face of different opportunities and constraints.

Thus the elements chosen to represent the brand must ideally have all the above six qualities or criteria.

These six qualities or criteria are explained here below:

1. **Memorable:** The brand elements should be such that they are easily recalled. To qualify as memorable the element should have the capability to be easily recognisable. Is the brand element recognisable at point of purchase as well as consumption? Short brand names usually have these criteria.

2. **Meaningful:** To what extend do the brand elements say something about the personality of the brand. Can the elements be associated with the functioning of the brand, or the target consumer, or an ingredient of the brand? For example, the meaning behind the brand name diet cola. It immediately brings to mind the person for whom it is meant.

3. **Likeability:** How appealing do the consumers find the brand element. Is it aesthetically appealing to the consumer? The brand element should be visually and verbally appealing to be likeable.

4. **Transferable:** Can new products in the same or different category be introduced under the same brand element? If the answer is yes the element has the criteria of transferability. To what extent does the particular element add to the brand equity across geographical boundaries?

5. **Adaptable:** Adaptable means to what extent is the element adaptable and updateable.

6. **Protectable:** Is the brand name legally and competitively protectable? Is it easy to copy? It is important that brand names become synonymous with product categories such as Xerox and Kleenex retain their trademark rights and not become generic.

4.5 Building, Measuring and Managing Brand Equity

4.5.1 Building Brand Equity

The essence of Brand building is to develop a loyal customer base. Marketers build brand equity by communicating the right information about the brand to the right consumers. This includes all information forwarded to the consumer about the brand at all content points whether initiated by the marketer or not. However, from the marketing managers point of view there are three sets of brand drivers and they are:

1. **The brand elements:** The initial choice of brand elements goes a long way in building the brand equity. Each element that is the brand name, logo, slogan, mascot, jingles, packages, signages and the spokespersons should communicate information about the brand that positively reinforces its functioning, composition or advantages. Brand elements play a number of brand building roles. Brand elements should be easily remembered, recognised and recalled. They should have the criteria as mentioned above in brand element criteria. Memorable or meaningful brand elements that create a complete story about the product in the mind of the consumer are the first step in building brand equity.

2. **Product or service and supporting marketing activities**: A proper choice of brand elements does go a long way in building brand equity. However the primary input for building brand equity comes from the actual product or service and the various supporting marketing activities.

Brands are not built only through advertising. They are built through all brand contacts. Brand contact has been defined by **Kotler** and **Keller** as "any information bearing experience a customer or prospect has with the brand, the product category, or the market that relates to the marketers product or service". Thus, every customers experience with a brand builds a positive or a negative impression about the brand. These experiences can come from an interaction with the personnel of the company, a salesman, an online experience, a payment transaction etc.

Marketers are using innovative strategies to create marketing activities where a contact with consumers becomes possible. Thus marketers organise trade shows, games and events, sponsor events, undertake press releases and public relations activities and undertake social cause marketing. All this is done to see that the brand becomes memorable, recognisable and recallable. Further all such marketing activities are undertaken to see that the right consumer has the right experience with the brand and the right perception is created in his/her mind.

3. **Other Associations Indirectly transferred to the brand by linking it to some other entity (a person, place or thing)/ Leveraging Secondary Associations:** The third and final way to build a brand is associating it with something or someone that is already in the memory of the consumer and conveys a particular meaning to the consumer. Thus the marketer may link the brand to a particular place that has certain relevance to the consumer by saying that the raw material for the product has been procured from that place. Or he may link the product/ service to a particular culture or game by sponsoring the same. The marketer may further use a particular personality to advertise the product thus extending the personality and the meaning it conveys to his own brand. Thus leveraging secondary associations is actually borrowing associations already in the memory of the consumer for your own brand by associating your brand with these people, places, events or things.

4.5.2 Measuring Brand Equity

The power of a brand depends upon what the consumer thinks about the brand. Thus it may be said that the power of the brand resides in the mind of the consumer. There are two ways of measuring

1. The Direct Approach and 2. The Indirect Approach.
1. **The Direct Approach:** The direct approach assesses the impact of knowledge of the brand on the consumer's response to the various marketing activities related to the brand.
2. **The Indirect Approac**h: The Indirect approach assesses the consumers brand knowledge and on the basis of that tries to identify various sources of brand equity. Both the above approaches of measuring brand equity are complementary. The marketers can employ both.

4.5.3 Managing Brand Equity

A consumers' reaction to a marketing initiative depends upon the knowledge that he has about the brand. All marketing initiatives elicit a response. Any marketing initiative changes the knowledge that the consumer has about the brand and influences his response to future marketing initiatives. Thus the marketing initiates whether short term or long term are to be carefully designed so as to add an affirmative information about the brand in the mind of the consumer. Thus all marketing initiatives should be planned and undertaken keeping in mind a long term view and positive impact on the mind of the consumer

For brand equity to be effective, it has to last over a long period of time. The marketer must understand that all marketing activities undertaken to create brand equity, must be undertaken with the long-term objective in mind.

4.5.4 Linking Advertising and Sales Promotion to Achieve 'Brand-Standing'

Brand standing is a position that a brand occupies in the market. This position comes from the thought process of the consumer. What the consumer thinks about the brand comes from all his experiences with the brand. It comes from what each element of the brand speaks and the interpretation of this speech by the consumer. This thought process should be reinforced every time the consumer has a new experience with a brand, for example, a "Rado watch". It is an expensive watch and the ownership gives the user the feeling of being one among the elite class. All advertising and sales promotion activities of the particular brand should be such that they reinforce the brand position and standing. In fact it is a circular process. Depends upon which the consumer sees first. If the consumer becomes aware of a brand through its advertisement, then this advertisement creates a particular image about the brand in the mind of the consumer. The use of the product or the interaction of the consumer with the brand should reinforce this image or take it to a next positive level. That is the brand standing should increase. Similarly, if the consumer interacts with the brand for the first time through a sales promotion activity, this interaction will create an image about the brand in the mind of the consumer and all further interactions with the brand should reinforce this image and take it to the next positive level. Thus all promotional activities undertaken to promote the brand should reinforce the brand placement and standing. They should be consistent with the image of the brand. For example, the type of events that Rado would sponsor should be in consistence with its image. A brand like Rado cannot afford to sponsor a small, negligible event. It would affect its brand standing. Further the advertisement and all elements of the advertisement should be of a posh nature in keeping with the image of the brand.

4.5.5 Leveraging Brand Values for Business and Non-business Contexts

The value of a brand is the amount a consumer is willing to pay for a product because it has a particular name as compared to what he is willing to pay for the product if it does not carry the particular name. The extra amount that the consumer is willing to pay is known as brand equity. It is this equity that gives value to the brand. The higher the brand equity the more valuable is the brand. A high value brand can be used to introduce new products. All products introduced under a high value brand are actually brand extensions. They automatically inherit the reputation of the original brand. Further, an organisation can use the value of a brand to demand more from all business intermediaries. For example, a higher value brand is capable of demanding more window space, exclusive showrooms, exclusive service centres etc. It places its owners in a position to demand the best services with all intermediaries. Further, the value of the brand can be redeemed in case the brand is to be sold. It will get a good amount for the owner. People like to work for well known brands. A higher value brand is capable of attracting the best talents to work for it. People are also willing to work for a lesser amount for a strong brand.

There are various ways that the value of a brand can be leveraged in a non-business context. The average human being is desirous of being upwardly mobile in a social situation. Thus he is always aspiring for better things in life. Further the average human being is respectful of the rich and the better things in life. Owning a high value brand will gain you respect from the average human being. It automatically opens doors which remain shut for lower brands.

Points to Remember

- **Sales promotion** means the steps that are taken for the purpose of obtaining an increasing sale". Often this term refers specially to selling efforts that are designed to supplement personal selling and advertising and by co-ordination helps them to become more effective.

- **Cross promotion** is a form of advertising that involves two or more parties. It is a way in which two parties help each other to promote each other's product. It is also is used by organisations to stand out from their competition in a crowded advertising marketplace. They are used by businesses, non-profit government agencies to "outmarket" bigger competitors.

- **Surrogate advertising** is a sort of advertising where a cover product is promoted in order to promote the actual product that is banned. A surrogate advertising campaign can be used to indirectly promote products or services deemed by some groups as being unhealthy, unethical, and immoral or, possibly, illegal through activities that are viewed as acceptable forms of promotion.

- **Bait and switch advertising** is a common form of false advertising. It occurs when a seller advertises a bargain on an item to attract a customer to the store.

- A **Brand** is a name, term, sign, symbol, or design or a combination of these, intended to identify the goods or services of one seller or a group of sellers and to differentiate them from those of the competitors.

- **Brand Name** is that part that can be spoken. This includes letters, words and numbers. Brand names simplify shopping, guarantee a certain level of quality and allow for self-expression.

- **Brand Mark** is the element of the brand that cannot be spoken, for example, symbol.

- **Trademark** is a legal designation that the owner has exclusive rights to the brand or part of a brand.

- **Trade Name** is the full legal name of the organisation, not the name of a specific product.

- **Brand equity** is the higher value that a company can get on the sale of a branded product as compared to a generic product.

- **Brand elements** are those trademarkable devices that serve to identify and differentiate the brand.

Questions for Discussion

1. Explain the meaning of sales promotion.
2. What are the objectives of sales promotion?
3. Elaborate the different techniques of sales promotion.
4. What is branding? Explain in detail.
5. Describe and explain the importance of brand equity.

■ ■ ■

Chapter 5...

Role of Information Technology in Advertising and Sales Promotion

Contents ...

Learning Objectives ...

- To discuss the role of IT in advertising and sales promotion
- To compare traditional and modern advertising
- To explain the purpose, types, advantages and disadvantages of internet advertising
- To understand the pre-requisites of online advertising
- To have an overview of internet advertising today

5.1 Role of IT in Advertising and Sales Promotion

Information technology is a term which talks about the techniques, methods and systems that we use for sharing information with others. Information technology is also being used when it comes to advertising a product or service. Information technology is helping the advertising industry to improve its performance by increasing sales and thereby increasing the profit margin of companies.

The revolution of Information technology that initiated during last decade of the 20th century has continued right through the commencement of the new millennium. It has changed the world in all facets. Information technology development and the wonderful phenomenon of Internet have given a new dimension to the human life and work. Amongst the various scientific disciplines that have developed under the influence of changes in the IT sector, a significant place belongs to marketing. Advertisements are of many types and this includes online advertisement, TV commercials, radio advertisements, and even emails. Almost every form of communication that we have today may be used to advertise a product or a service.

When you open your facebook or twitter account, you will see an advertisement and if you like it, you tend to click on it. This is exactly how marketers use information technology to advertise their products or services. Internet based advertising is a very cheap option in contrast to advertising through televisions and other media. This is because internet has a much larger audience from where an advertiser can direct his advertisements to the right recipient. The targeting of audience also becomes easy because the advertiser can easily reach out to his target market as they have some common websites they will visit thus further reducing the cost of advertising through the internet. The advantages that information technology has brought to marketing and sales industry is evident as advertisers are able to endorse their products more easily yet effectively.

One of the greatest authors in marketing, Philip Kotler, believes that "The intense technological progress and the use of Internet have made so-called "new economy", which will outdate many marketing strategies, like mass marketing. At the same time, the need for the development of new strategies is being born, which will adapt better to the modern environment and growing demands of the world market"

Communication within various disciplines and subjects on the market has been enhanced and facilitated by the Internet, because irrespective of where a person is, everyone is just one click away from the rest of the world. Closeness of such a magnitude was achieved never before in the history of mankind, this probably shows the largest contribution that Internet, as the new technology, has brought to the world.

5.2 Comparison of Traditional and Modern Advertising

We are living in a modern world with modern technology which has eventually resulted in a modern approach to marketing. However the question arises, what about traditional marketing? Is there still scope for it?

Let us take a moment to get a little boring and define traditional advertising. Traditional advertising deals with use of material such as, brochures, business cards, leaflets, billboard advertising, newspaper, magazine, fuel station, telemarketing, sales letters etc. the list just goes on.

The traditional advertising approach has been working all these years because that was just what customers wanted, this was how they wanted to be contacted regarding products. Actually these were the only ways that the seller could contact the buyer. Soon the Internet came in, and now we found out that we could communicate with a much wider audience simultaneously and this opened up a new vehicle for advertising.

Now bouncing back to the original question what about traditional advertising? We still buy magazines, we still visit fuel stations and we still receive newspapers and leaflets through the door. So does that mean traditional advertising still has scope?

So let's compare the two i.e. Traditional advertising and Modern advertising

Sr. No.	Basis of Distinction	Traditional Advertising	Modern Advertising
1.	Communication	Traditional advertising is a form of one way communication i.e. from Marketer to customer	Modern advertising is a form of two way communication i.e. from Marketer to customer and customer to Marketer
2.	Transparency	Traditional advertising is not transparent and has a lot of partial or incomplete information	Modern advertising is pretty transparent and usually has all the information clearly disclosed.
3.	Target Audience	Traditional advertising targets mass markets. It tries to target the entire population in one go.	Modern advertising targets one-on-one marketing strategy. They make ads which create interest in the minds of the viewer.
4.	About	In Traditional advertising it's all about the seller.so it's just 'about me'. It contains details of what the seller wants to sell.	In modern advertising it's about the seller as well as the buyer it's 'about us'. It contains details of what the seller wants to sell and is related to what the buyer wants to buy.
5.	Content	In Traditional advertising the content is usually rigid and polished. It gives a larger than life picture of the advertisement.	In modern advertising the content is more flexible and authentic. The content is created keeping the brand and its user in mind.

contd. ...

6.	**Cost**	Usually the cost of traditional media is high when compared to modern media.	Usually the cost of modern media is low when compared to traditional media.
7.	**Reach**	The reach of traditional media is limited.	The reach of modern media is huge and effective.
8.	**Control over communication**	Traditional media being a one way street is more controlled and rigid.	Modern media being a two way street is more unstructured and free.
9.	**Scheduling**	In traditional media the contents of the advertisement are pre-produced and scheduled.	In modern media the contents are created real time.
10.	**Language**	The language used in traditional media is very formal	The language used in modern media is informal in natural.
11.	**Customer involvement**	Traditional media being a one way street the customer involvement is passive and limited.	Modern media being a two way street there is active customer involvement.

5.3 Internet Advertising

5.3.1 Introduction

Internet advertising is a marketing strategy that involves the use of the Internet as a medium to obtain website traffic and target and deliver marketing messages to the right customers. Online advertising is geared toward defining markets through unique and useful applications. Internet advertising is also known as online advertising.

Advertisements to be released on the internet are easy to prepare and a lot many courses on web page designing are available today. You also have many web page designers who compete with each other for the client's businesses. The cost of preparing an internet advertisement is much less as compared to the price paid for the preparation of a television advertisement or for the hire of a prime hoarding. Further, internet advertisements can result in immediate action as a person accessing the internet can make a direct online purchase. Thus, the effectiveness of the internet advertisement can be measured.

However, an advertisement on the internet has to compete with various other advertisements for the attention of the viewer. It also has to compete with the contents of the web page for which the viewer had originally accessed the internet. He definitely did not access it to view advertisements. Thus, the internet advertisement has to be very attractive as the viewer is conscious of the time he is spending on the internet. This is because accessing the internet costs money and this has to be paid in terms of amount of time spent on the internet. Thus, in order to catch the attention of the viewer, advertisements on the internet are basically used as vehicles that carry sales promotion messages. Thus, you will find most advertisements on the internet with words like Free, 40% Discount, Money Back Offer, in order to lure the viewer towards viewing it, and take immediate buying decisions. Sometimes, the internet advertisements take a lot of time to download, and hence, miss the attention of the viewer totally.

However, today is the era of the internet and information technology. People over the world are beginning to rely more and more on the internet due to its wide accessibility. In fact, its popularity is such that people are beginning to become internet addicts. Once used to it, you just cannot do without it. In other words, if you have a computer at home, today you can do away with the television as well as the music system. In the households of the future, the internet will be replacing the television and, hence, the importance of internet advertising is projected to occupy a very 'dominant' place in the future.

5.3.2 Purpose of Internet Advertising

We all know that the days of offline marketing are numbered. Online advertising is rapidly becoming the prime area of concentration of every marketer. All the top-notch advertising firms such as Ogilvie and Mudra, JWT, FCB Ulka, Marther and the like have started separate verticals specialising in online advertising for their agencies. Whether a business is small or big, online advertising has proven to be extremely beneficial for it. It not only gets you long term value, but also ensures that every rupee you pay is worth it. Let's look at the purpose behind online advertising:

1. **Wider Reach:** Majority of online advertisements work on the principle of geometric progression, which means it not only gets notified to your network, but also in the network of your friend and in your friend's friend network too. Hence, Even 1% conversion of your total reach will make your business swell and lead to huge profits. A wider reach will not only help in increasing sales, but also create awareness about the brand.

2. **Targets the Niche Market:** While majority of businesses have products for masses, some companies target a very niche audience. Internet Advertisement gives the freedom to choose the target group that the company aim to reach to. It is particularly critical for businesses, which offer high value products. A company may target its audience based on a variety of parameters such as geographical area, age, education, income, religion, interests and nationality among others.

3. **Inexpensive as compared to other Mediums:** Online advertisements are very inexpensive when compared to the offline counterparts. The best part of online advertising is that you can pay according to your advertising budget. There are various options available in regards to making payment. The two most popular payment methods are known as CPM (Cost Per Impression) and CPC (Cost Per Click). Both are effective but the company needs to find out which one works best for their business.

4. **Easy Measurability of Investment:** Gone are the days when companies used to spend huge amounts of money hoping that their brand will get noticed and their products or services will be sold. In the digital era, a company can actually measure its investment and get a quantitative report on each campaign on which money was spent. The quantified data of numbers and charts will help the company understand which campaign is working for them and which ones are best to get rid of.

5. **Creating Brand Awareness:** While selling is the most important function of advertising, creating brand awareness is all the more important keeping the long term benefits in mind. Online advertisement is a perfect tool that makes people aware about the brand. It makes more sense for smaller businesses to opt for internet advertising as compared to the more conventional types of advertisements.

6. **Cost of Acquisition per Customer:** Internet advertisement ensures that the cost of acquisition per customer is very less as compared to other mediums. It is a simple equation, lesser the cost higher the profit. It makes more sense to spend online especially when the overhead costs of the company are high.

7. **The Way Forward:** With a rapid increase in penetration of the internet, the business benefits will only go on increasing. Not to mention the smart phones and tablets have made internet more easily accessible than before.

5.3.3 Types of Internet Advertising

1. **Website Banner Advertisements:** Web Banner Advertising is a type of Internet advertising whereby you pay another website 'X' amount to display an advertising banner on their website for a certain length of time. The web banner links directly to your website, tempting visitors away from theirs and onto yours. Sometimes, advertising on another website in the form of a banner advertisement can yield a fairly good return. However, advertising on a website that has little or nothing to do with your target audience involves high levels of luck to convert any sales, producing little to no return on investment (ROI).

Stylishly done banner ad campaigns will continue to be the staple of internet advertising for the immediate future. Studies show that banners are terribly good at generating traffic through click-throughs and have a powerful branding effect.

Matching site content to banner advertising subject can certainly increase their power. Selecting a banner, to display based on the observed personal preferences and interests of a visitor, is a extremely powerful sales tool. The potential for targeted banners is huge.

2. **Sponsorships:** If you 'sponsor' a section of a site you can integrate your advertising message and branding elements a bit more unobtrusively than you can with just a banner at the top. You might also be able to have your regular ads and have "these cool pages sponsored by ..." appear on the pages you're sponsoring. Thus, you may get more exposure and closer integration with content.

3. **Rich Media:** Right now, this term seems to mean a more or less normal-sized banner ad that uses Java, HTML or any other software to make the advertisement have dropdown boxes, wiggly bits, sound on mouse-over, small games etc. Both visitors and sites like them because you don't have to actually leave the site to interact with the banner. Click-through on such advertisements can be quite high.

4. **Text Link Exchanges and Paid Link Advertising:** In more recent times, link exchanges have become quite popular. The general idea is, two like-minded websites exchange a contextually based link (text link), normally placed on a dedicated resources page which is linked from every page of the site. Webmasters will approach another website of a similar theme to ask if they would exchange a link. The link can provide traffic from one site to the other.

   Link popularity: Many of the largest search engines use link popularity in their complex ranking algorithms. The idea being if a website is of good quality, other webmasters will link to it from their own site. Each web page has one vote, linking to another site is in effect casting that vote, if the page links to more than one site, the vote is diluted between each link. The other key part to conducting link exchanges is using keyword targeted descriptive text as the actual clickable part of the link (anchor text).

   Purchasing text links works exactly the same way as above apart from the fact that you purchase the link rather than exchange; you don't have to provide a link back either. Purchasing links will often lead to a link displayed in a more prominent place. The price of purchasing links depends on a number of criteria, such as, the amount of traffic on the site, and the Google Page Rank (PR) which is an indication of the weight a link would produce.

5. **Keyword Advertising:** This can be quite effective. What you do is pay a search engine, directory or site to have your ad or link to your site pop up first when someone does a search on the keywords you buy. When someone does a search using the word 'scales', your matter comes up on top of the list and/or your banner ad is at the top of the page. The best searched words like 'sex' and 'air transport' are

usually sold out or very expensive. The less-searched words are cheaper but can also bring a very valuable targeted person to your site. By now, everyone's heard about the old misspelling trick. If someone else has already bought the keyword 'hamburger', you could probably buy slight misspellings like, 'hmburger' or 'hamburgr' cheap that would still get you good action.

6. **Coupon Deals:** Web Advertisements carrying digital coupons that give you special deals for ecommerce purchases or printable coupons provide the advertiser the opportunity to do all the wonderful and horrible things traditionally possible with coupons, but now you can do it on the Web. Airlines are using these to increase their air traffic.

7. **Pay per Click or Pay per Sale:** Some sites sell space to advertisers. The advertisers have their banners or rich media advertisements on sites on which they have hired space. The advertiser pays the site only when someone clicks upon the banner or gets to the target site and buys something. Such advertisers pay a bit more to the site but the payment depends upon the number of clicks, or number of purchases, as the case may be. Such deals make people buying ads get a more secure return on their investment, Such deals are fine for the people buying the ads but do not tend to pay off well for the advertising sites, as some people will actually click on the ads and the site will lose them.

8. **Pop-up and Pop-under:** Pop-up and Pop-under are simply the forms of internet advertising available. A Pop-up displays an advertisement of a website in a new window when you visit another site; a Pop-under inserts the advertisement under the page you are viewing so that when you close the window down, you are presented with it.

   If you use the internet you're bound to have come across Pop-ups before and probably are already sick to death of them. Most of the time people see them loading up and they are able to close the window before they've fully loaded. In recent times, Pop-ups have become much less popular, as they are being made redundant by most browsers and downloadable toolbars like the Google toolbar and Microsoft IE, who are coming up with complete Pop-up blockers. However, these services are cheap and are sold mostly on the premise of people thinking, "Well, it's only £10 for a thousand, I may as well give it a try."

Thus, these are some of the different ways in which a company can use the internet or web pages to advertise its products or services.

5.3.4 Advantages of Internet Advertising

Internet advertising is inexpensive and reaches a wider audience and will probably be more profitable than traditional advertising. Internet advertising has a lot of advantages that traditional advertising does not. Internet advertising gives such amazing possibilities that it would put you in a dilemma: video advertising, e-mail advertising, banner advertising, mobile advertising, advertising on social networks, Google Search (SEO) advertising, and a lot more.

1. **Wider Reach:** Majority of online advertisements work on the principle of geometric progression, which means it not only gets notified to your network, but also in the network of your friend and in your friend's friend network too. Hence, Even 1% conversion of your total reach will make your business swell and lead to huge profits. A wider reach will not only help in increasing sales, but also create awareness about the brand

2. **Targets the Niche Market:** While majority of businesses have products for masses, some companies target a very niche audience. Internet Advertisement gives the freedom to choose the target group that the company aim to reach to. It is particularly critical for businesses, which offer high value products. A company may target its audience based on a variety of parameters such as geographical area, age, education, income, religion, interests and nationality among others.

3. **Measureable results:** Gone are the days when companies used to spend huge amounts of money hoping that their brand will get noticed and their products or services will be sold. In the digital era, a company can actually measure its investment and get a quantitative report on each campaign on which money was spent. The quantified data of numbers and charts will help the company understand which campaign is working for them and which ones are best to get rid of.

4. **Brand Awareness:** While selling is the most important function of advertising, creating brand awareness is all the more important keeping the long term benefits in mind. Online advertisement is a perfect tool that makes people aware about the brand. It makes more sense for smaller businesses to opt for internet advertising as compared to the more conventional types of advertisements.

5. **Affordable:** Internet advertisement ensures that the cost of acquisition per customer is very less as compared to other mediums. It is a simple equation, lesser the cost higher the profit. It makes more sense to spend online especially when the overhead costs of the company are high.

6. **Speed:** Internet advertising is much faster than any of the other offline advertising counterparts and the company can start sending out its online ads to a larger audience, as soon as it starts its advertising campaign. If the company has a very big target market online at the time of triggering the online advertisements, then the advertisement will be served to majority of the company's target market instantly.

7. **Informative:** In Internet advertising, the advertiser is capable of conveying more details about the advertisement to the target audience and that too at very low cost. Majority of the Internet Advertising campaigns are of a click-able link to a specific target page, where the user gets information in detail about the products mentioned in the advertisement.

8. **Flexible Payment:** Online advertisements are very inexpensive when compared to the offline counterparts. The best part of online advertising is that you can pay according to your advertising budget. In offline advertising the company needs to pay the complete amount to the advertising agency irrespective of the ad campaign results. In Internet Advertising there is a flexibility of paying only for qualified leads, clicks or impressions. There are various options available in regards to making payment. The two most popular payment methods are known as CPM (Cost Per Impression) and CPC (Cost Per Click). Both are effective but the company needs to find out which one works best for their business.

9. **Better ROI:** Since payment for Internet Advertising is performance based, the company is bound to have a better ROI when compared with offline advertising. The company can also easily track and analyse the performance of its online advertisements and adjust them so as to improve its ROI.

10. **Easy Audience Engagement:** Most of the internet advertisement platforms make it easy for the audience to engage with the advertisement of the products. As an advertiser the company would be able to get a clear feedback from the audience and thereby help in improving the quality of advertisements.

The benefits and advantages of internet advertising are not confined to the above mentioned points, one may come up with more valuable points in this regards.

5.3.5 Disadvantages of Internet Advertising

The increased reach potential of internet advertising is also argued to be one of its downfalls. For example, the Internet is massive and competitive and it's unlikely that the online advertisement will be seen beyond readers of a particular website. Moreover, Internet advertising is easy to ignore or skip when compared to a hard copy magazine or newspaper. It is rightly said that every coin has two sides. After seeing the pros of internet advertising let us look at the flip side of advertising on the internet. Internet advertising suffers from serious security issues and copyright problems.

1. **Interrupting advertisements:** A lot of internet advertising campaigns are intrusive in nature, that's why browsers have pop-up blocker options that frequently prevent ads from popping up. Almost all browsers block pop-ups automatically. The web browsers such as Chrome, Opera and Firefox now have extensions available which block ads on websites. More and more customers are using these methods to avoid seeing so many advertisements.

2. **Copyright problem:** Due to internet advertising the companies advertising material is automatically available for everyone across the world. Competitors can copy it, regardless of the legal ramifications. Trademarks, pictures and logos can be copied and used for commercial purposes, unlike traditional advertising such as TV, radio and newspaper in which copying the content was a very difficult task.

3. **Customers Ignore Ads:** Due to bombarding of advertisements consumers have gotten used to seeing advertisements on television, hearing radio commercials and flipping through magazine ads, they've developed a type of immunity to all forms of advertising. This has also become the case with online advertising, where consumers are avoiding to click banner advertisements, bypassing ads in online videos and close pop-up advertisements as soon as they pop up on the screens. Customers are in total control of which advertisements they want to click and respond to.

4. **Viewing issues:** Lag in website or video loading and problems with the browser can reduce the frequency with which the consumers see online advertisements. When technical problems come up, companies lose the opportunity of broadcasting the advertisements of their products and services and there are chances of losing potential sales. Viewing problems may occur due to problems with a website or if a customer is using a smart phone or other mobile devices to view a website, the speed of internet connection also plays a vital role. Viewing issues may also crop up due to the user not having the correct applications and programs installed on his computer for proper viewing.

5. **Consumers Get Distracted:** When a customer visit a website, he usually has a goal in mind, whether it's to catch up on the latest gossip, read the news, chat with friends, use social media, download music or may be shop for a specific item. Internet advertisements at this point of time can easily distract the customer and pull his attention off the online advertisements.

6. **Advertising overload:** Every advertiser keeps craving for consumers' attention, and with the introduction of Internet advertising there is just too much information to digest. The solution is to develop creative advertisement campaigns that will rip through the clutter of advertisements and strike an emotional chord with your target audience.

7. **Difficulty in Measuring Effectiveness:** Measuring the effectiveness and reach of internet advertising involves evaluating complex, sets of metrics. Even after crunching the numbers and looking at how many sales have been converted from the advertisements, it is difficult to connect the dots and tell the entire story of how effectively the message got across. A lot of factors contribute to the success of the advertisement right from how you pay for your ads -- by the click or by the sale, to where your ads appear (as in which website) plays a role in how well your online outreach works.

8. **Too Many Options:** The Internet has a wide range of websites on which companies can place their advertisements. This can be overpowering, especially for small business houses. With so many options to choose from, it is difficult to narrow down

on the choice of websites that will attract potential customers and lead to sales. Once an organisation selects a website, the next challenge is the variety of ways in which one can advertise its products or services on the site, for example through banner advertisements, video marketing, pop-ups or sponsoring a post. Companies need to statistically determine which type of advertisement yields the best response from their target markets.

9. **Click Fraud:** Depending on how the company pays for its internet advertising, the company may encounter a common form of fraud based on inflated click rates. If the company's ad placement costs rely on the number of clicks its advertisement messages receive, then the competitor can pay a small sum of money and hire people to inflate the click rate and drive up the costs for your company.

5.4 Pre-Requisites of Online Advertising and E-Advertising Guidelines

The massive global reach of the internet makes it an attractive option for the marketers and company's wishing to advertise its products. To get a complete understanding of the regulations related to online advertising, even in just one country, such as the USA we will need to take account of the different sources, which provide us with a huge range of rules to consider. There is no one point or place where we can get all the rules. Since the online world deals with dissemination and use of a broad range of information, covering a large range of issues and matters, any rules on the broadcasting of information might be applicable. The rules and regulations that regulate the online world may be pervasive applying to any, range of activities. The rules laid down in the Data Protection Act 1998 or the Trade Descriptions Act 1968 would be an apt example.

Pre-requisites of Online Advertising/E-Advertising Guidelines

1. **Develop Relevant and Valuable Content**

    Content is king in the world of digital marketing. On the other hand, it should always add value, be so convincing that it gets your customers talking, and so good that it needs to be shared with others. A few examples:

    - Provide high-quality infographics that drive traffic and generate connections to your website.

    - Publish free guides or white papers that help your clients without giving away your proprietary processes.

    - Make interviews with Key opinion leaders and other recognised experts available- an easy way to build great content while positioning you as the go-to professional.

2. **Optimise your website with SEO**

   Successful digital marketing needs you to be updated with the changing demographics and informed about your customer's behaviour and preferences. Steps to be a successful SEO:
   - Know your target audience and the kind of information they normally search for.
   - Identify the most important keywords and use them to optimise your website.
   - Continually reassess and improve your SEO.

3. **Initiate dynamic customer interactions across various social channels**

   Unless you use your digital marketing resources to involve your customers in productive communication, it can be hard to capture their attention. You need to:
   - Broaden your reach and promote your content through social media.
   - Grow your subscriber base and change site traffic into leads.
   - Nurture your leads and leverage customer loyalties through word of mouth.
   - Keep the conversations going.

4. **Transform your digital marketing with mobility**

   The use of mobile platforms is changing customer behaviour and giving us new and unmatched digital marketing opportunities. A few examples of mobile tools:
   - SMS alerts
   - QR codes
   - Mobile website optimisation
   - Apps
   - Augmented reality
   - Location-based advertising

5. **Utilise Big Data to make better digital marketing decisions**

   Consumers use many digital and social mediums, and communicate with these in several different ways and for different reasons, which considerably affects your digital marketing strategy. If used properly, big data can help you to:
   - Leverage new tools and technical know-how to involve your customers, subscribers and viewers across all channels.
   - Increase the conversion rate of lead-to-client with customer relationship management, automation management, reporting and data governance.

6. **Build your brand with high-quality webinars and live events**

   Use your digital marketing resources to engage with your customers, build trust, and increase your brand awareness. Try to create a flawless brand experience. A few examples:
   - Webinars
   - Podcasts
   - Use email or twitter to invite your customers to live events in their regional area
   - Promote tradeshows and conferences

7. **Create an attractive-looking ad**.

   The goal is to attract a potential customer. To do so, limit the amount of words in your ad, have an image that appeals to the customers, create a headline that draws people in, and guide them to a clear and easy call to action.

8. **Be intentional in your design.**

   What do you hope to achieve with your ad? Is it to promote your brand, to generate interest, or to teach? Is it to generate sales, and if so, how will that occur? What do you want the individual looking at your ad to do? Don't try to do too much—try to implement one strategy at a time.

9. **Create a sense of need.**

   Why should anyone respond to your ad? What's in it for them? What solution(s) does your product provide?

10. **Don't communicate too much**.

    It is clear that you are passionate about your products and you want everyone to know every characteristic and advantage your product provides. But if you try to incorporate in excess, people will just move on from your ad and will not want to read all you have to say.

11. **Keep the message simple.**

    "Your advertising should offer one particular advantage that the customer will like by calling you, by coming to your organisation or by using your product or service. A seven-year-old child should be capable of looking at your advertisement and explain to another seven-year-old just what you are offering and why it is attractive to a future customer. If your advertisement does not pass the "seven-year-old test," modify it and rewrite it until it does."

12. **Plan your marketing efforts with a multi-stage strategy**.

    When campaigns are combined with both digital and print advertising then, it is 34 percent more effective. Connect with your target audience using various media platforms. Your customers get their information from many sources; the more places they see your firm's products, the more open they will be to them.

5.5 Internet Advertising Today

The customer today, unlike yesteryears is a smart and sharp minded person, he knows a great ad as soon as he sees one, but getting that ad across to right kind of people at the right time is a task in itself. As there is innovation in advertising technology it is leading to obsolescence of old tactics, and is also opening up new opportunities to reach the target audience.

1. **Mobile video advertising:** Mobile video consumption is growing rapidly and providing advertisers with a way to reach consumers when they are paying attention. With the evolution of smartphones and tablet video consumption has grown by 400 percent and now accounts for more than 30 percent of all online videos played, according to Ooyala's Global Video Index.

   This trend has been assisted by the expansion of super fast 3G and 4G networks. The popularity of 'phablets' (large-screen smartphones) also mirrors the growing importance of mobile video.

   Mobile video viewers are also called as "captive" audience. When there is a commercial break on TV, people look down at their phones. When travelling, people focus on their cellphone screens and phablets instead of the ads passing by in the cityscape. When there is a radio ad, people change the radio station. However, when people are already looking into their smartphones, nothing is going to distract them and they will give 100% attention to the advertisement.

2. **Smart Phone apps. advertisement:** Smart Phone apps advertising is a form of advertising through mobile phones or other mobile devices. It is a subcategory of mobile marketing. It is estimated that by ads on mobile apps account for 30% of all mobile advertising revenue in 2014, and will top $4.6bn in 2015, and over $6.8bn by the end of 2019.

   It is very much possible that advertisers and media industry will take account of a bigger and faster growing mobile app market, though it remains at a meager 1% of global advertising spend. Mobile media is evolving very fast and while mobile phones will continue to be the most important, it is not clear whether mobile phones based on cellular networks or smartphones based on WiFi will prevail. Nonetheless, such is the emergence of this form of advertising, that there is now a dedicated global awards ceremony organised every year by Visiongain.

   According to a recent survey Mobile phones outnumber TV sets by over 3 to 1, and PC based internet users by 4 to 1, and the total laptop and desktop PC population by nearly 5 to 1, advertisers in many markets have recently rushed to this media.

3. **Social Media Advertising:** With the social media apps and super-fast internet connections the social media has become a hot spot for advertisers who are searching for their target customers Social networks like facebook, Twitter, whatsapp etc have been a great source of advertising vehicles. Infact some businesses thrive only on the basis of social media advertising as it is free and has a great reach.

4. **Search Engine Marketing (SEM):** Search engine marketing is a type of marketing that seeks to promote websites by increasing its visibility in SERPs (Search Engine Result Pages). SEM tactics include contextual advertising, paid placement, and paid inclusion, at times it also includes free SEO (Search Engine Optimization) techniques

to drive placement of their ads. Advertisers pay each time users click on their listing and are redirected to their website, rather than for the ad itself. This system allows brands to refine searches and gain information about their market.

5. **Affiliate marketing:** Affiliate marketing is a type of online advertising where the advertisers place his campaign with a potentially large number of publishers, who are paid media fees only when the advertiser receives traffic on his website. This is usually accomplished through contracting with an affiliate network.

6. **Blog advertising:** These days most of internet users have blogs, these are personal blogs through which they try to advertise their products to make profit. This strategy works if you manage to produce something different with your blog which can attract the readers. Blog advertising is best fit for new launches, new products, and newsmakers.

Points to Remember

- Internet advertising is a marketing strategy that involves the use of the Internet as a medium to obtain website traffic and target and deliver marketing messages to the right customers.

- Web Banner Advertising is a type of Internet advertising whereby you pay another website 'X' amount to display an advertising banner on their website for a certain length of time.

- A Pop-up displays an advertisement of a website in a new window when you visit another site; a Pop-under inserts the advertisement under the page you are viewing so that when you close the window down, you are presented with it.

- Search engine marketing is a type of marketing that seeks to promote websites by increasing its visibility in SERPs (Search Engine Result Pages).

- Affiliate marketing is a type of online advertising where the advertisers place his campaign with a potentially large number of publishers, who are paid media fees only when the advertiser receives traffic on his website.

Questions for Discussion

1. Discuss the role of IT in advertising and sales promotion.
2. Compare traditional and modern advertising.
3. Explain the purpose, types, advantages and disadvantages of internet advertising.
4. Describe the pre-requisites of online advertising.
5. Give an overview of internet advertising today.

■■■

www.ingramcontent.com/pod-product-compliance
Lightning Source LLC
Chambersburg PA
CBHW080730020726
47503CB00010B/2866